MW00462137

Call Back Yesterday

James D. Forman

Call Back Yesterday

Charles Scribner's Sons | New York

Library of Congress Cataloging in Publication Data
Forman, James D. Call back yesterday.
Summary: An American girl, sole survivor of the violent climax to the terrorist takeover of an American embassy, tries, with a doctor's help, to piece together her memory of the crucial incident in time to avert a world conflict.
[1. Terrorism—Fiction] I. Title.
PZ7.F76Cal [Fic] 81-14416
ISBN 0-684-17168-6 AACR2

This book published simultaneously in the United States of America and in Canada—

3 5 7 9 11 13 15 17 19 F/C 20 18 16 14 12 10 8 6 4 2

Printed in the United States of America

For Tuan Jim
in the hope that, come 1988,
he will frequent fertilizer factories
rather than foreign embassies

O, call back yesterday, bid time return . . .
King Richard the Second: III, ii

Call Back Yesterday

1

TAPE CRC 1: 7–27–88: 1:45 hours.
Subject: Cynthia Randall Cooper. Condition: guarded, shock, probable concussion. Severe lacerations left forearm. Moderate blood loss. Self-inflicted?

Cindy rose through cold and empty darkness into weak light, the moon seen through fog. She stirred, gave a faint cry. The moon solidified into a fluorescent panel directly overhead. Windowless walls closed around her. How had she come here? In a dazzling instant of clarity she saw the walls shatter into splinters of glass, an icy cascade flying toward her, and she screamed in utter silence as a dolphin must scream when crushed by the ocean depths. Abruptly she went blind to the scene; the walls reestablished themselves. Her head pounded. She could scarcely breathe. "Help me," she tried to articulate, making only animal sounds. "Daddy, help me, please." There was no one there. So weak. Even moving her head was painful, but that was enough to show her a bottle of clear fluid hanging from a stainless-steel hook. A plastic tube descended from the bottle to her bandaged right arm, which throbbed with pain. Her left wrist was heavily bandaged as well, and from the way her body felt beneath the taut sheet it must have been bruised all over. "Please, I want to go home now," she said, sounding like a baby just experimenting with words.

As though summoned a stranger entered the room. He seemed not so much to enter as to materialize: a rippling wave, real and unreal, seen through trick glass. He bent close, his head strangely circled with light, like a saint. Gazing steadily into her eyes, as if to physically hold her attention, he said, "I'm Doctor Harper. How are you feeling now? Can you tell me what happened, Cynthia?" His voice was slow and concerned, reminding Cindy of her father. Still, something inside registered danger, told her to say nothing. "You're looking much better, Cynthia. Are you feeling better?" the doctor said, and turned on a tape recorder.

"Dying?" she blurted back, a near shout. "Am I dying?" The words all ran together.

"Pardon?"

"Am I dying, Doctor?" She tried so hard to enunciate and still he did not seem to comprehend. "Home, let me go home." With a concentrated effort Cindy forced her lips to expell the word: "Dying?"

"Dying?" Doctor Harper leaned closer. "Oh my, no, you're in good hands here. You've lost some blood, Cynthia, but don't worry, we'll fix you up right as rain."

Rain? Did it ever rain in Arabia? In Switzerland there had been snow, safe, surrounding snow, and the mountains. She felt so tired yet suddenly talkative, not caring whether she made sense. It was like the Christmas party when the forbidden vodka had made her giddy. She began talking about the party, then stopped suddenly, feeling that something unalterable, something terrible that could not be undone had happened. "Doctor?" A hoarse clear whisper.

"Yes?" Again he was leaning close.

"What's wrong with me? What's happened?"

"That's exactly what we have to find out," he replied,

"as soon as you're well enough to help us." He bestowed a kindly, somewhat professional smile. "Meanwhile, you're not to worry. We're going to take good care of you. Hungry?"

"Tired," she replied. Her head felt ready to burst.

The doctor produced a small plastic cylinder from his pocket, removed the round lid, and extracted a translucent yellow capsule. From a chrome tap in the corner he filled a paper cup with water. "For your headache," he said. She did not resist as he helped her raise her head enough to wash down the pill.

"There," he said. "You rest now. And trust me. We'll see this through."

"Yes, please," Cindy barely whispered back, the mists already beginning to swirl. She needed someone to trust, someone to look after her.

"7–27–88: 8:30 hours," Harper informed the tape recorder. "End of tape CRC 2."

Cynthia Cooper's eyes were closed, her breathing erratic as though in the grip of a nightmare. "Poor kid, I wouldn't be in your skin for all the tea in China," Harper said aloud, and then quietly left the room that, with its small solitary patient, might have passed for an expensive veterinarian's operating theater.

2

Cindy stirred, opened her eyes. Doctor Harper was there watching her. "Have I been asleep or have we been talking all along?" she asked. Her words were clearer now, almost normal, but she knew she wasn't complete inside. It was as though some of the wires between then and now—not all, but many joining the present with the past—had been severed. She knew, too, now that she was awake, aware of the crisp white sheets, the bandages and the needle in her arm, that she did not want to explore backward into those dreams of screaming, of shattering glass, of being helpless and trapped. She needed to stay awake clutching the real sheets, feeling the real pain.

At exactly 13:00 hours, July 27, 1988, Doctor Harper switched on the tape recorder for the third time. "Better?" he asked.

Cindy didn't answer. She was sore all over and still terribly weak, yet at the same time restless and irritated to the point of bitchiness.

"What's going on here? What am I doing here? What is this place, anyway?" she demanded in a flood of questions.

"I'm glad to see you're taking an interest in your surroundings," Harper replied. "Your vital signs are coming along very well. Perhaps you'd care to eat something." Cindy noticed the trolley with the plastic tray. “No, thank you,” she said, with a push for emphasis. The table rolled silently back a couple of inches.

“You need to build your strength, Cynthia.”

“Cindy,” she corrected him. “And I’m not eating when I don’t know where I am or what I’m doing.”

“Easy,” he replied. “This is a hospital room. You’re my patient.”

“That’s no answer.”

“Sorry,” he said. “Slow down, okay? Leave the questions to me for a bit, and we’ll sort things out together. I promise. Can you tell me something about what went on before you came here?”

“What went on where?” Her head was pounding again, her pulse drummed danger.

“At the Embassy, in Riyadh. You could be a great help.”

“Why can’t I see my parents?”

“Because they aren’t here right now. Can you tell me about the Embassy?”

Waves of panic, things seen and not seen through a sort of fearful fog.

“Let’s go back, then. Get things in order, one step at a time. What do you say, Cindy?”

“Why hasn’t this hospital room any windows?”

The doctor ignored this. “You’re a student, isn’t that right? In Switzerland?”

Cindy felt too exhausted to resist. She sensed no threat here. “Yes, at Le Rosey.”

“That’s a very fine school.”

“I guess.”

“Not far from Geneva. Now, normally at Christmas you went back to the States?”

“My grandparents.”

"But this time you went to Saudi Arabia."

Cindy nodded, though she knew she was being drawn into peril.

"I'm surprised you went, what with the political situation so serious."

"Serious?" She hadn't known it was serious at the time, not like the war in South Africa or the bloody grain riots in India.

"Did you have official permission?"

"I don't know. I guess not exactly." Cindy was trying hard to recall but the pleasant memories were flooding back now. She remembered the end of the autumn term and the snow beginning to fall on the village of Rolle and the lake, and Mont Blanc rising up behind all the other mountains. Mountains made her feel secure. It had been a good term. She had won the school tennis prize before the snow came, and with school about to recess for Christmas, an art prize as well. Monsieur Reardon had held her small painting at arm's length, then leaned it against the wall for a longer look. "So you did this yourself, Mademoiselle Cooper? No one helped you?" And when she had said no with embarrassed pleasure he added, "Then why do you waste so much time with the tennis?" to which she had answered that art wasn't everything. "It should be, for you." Trying to please him, Cindy had said she'd be going to art school presently, and to his, "When?" she'd said, "The summer holidays." "Serious painters never have holidays," he'd informed her gravely.

That exchange had been sufficient to give her wings for a week, that and the big check from her grandmother, and the snow falling and melting and then beginning to stick until the dark buildings of Rolle wore white beards and caps. She could hear the endless sigh of the flakes against the wire of the tennis courts and remembered thrusting her hands down into the snow like a baker making bread. It had all been so lovely that suddenly she became unbearably sad and began to cry.

"What's wrong?" Doctor Harper asked. Oh, God. He'd seen so many hospital beds, so many pinched, bewildered faces appealing for the sort of help he could not give. For a moment he felt too tired to react, then braced himself to give comfort. "It's all right," he said, and took a tissue to wipe her eyes. "I wish it were easy, Cindy. I wish I could explain everything away with happy endings. But it's got to come from you, when you're ready."

Cindy shook her head back and forth slowly, blinded now with the tears. "I wish I could remember. You don't know how much." But with the wish came the obliterating fear.

Gently he brushed her hair back. "Take your time. Rest now, Cindy. Just take your time." Again came the cup of water and the yellow capsule. "You'll feel better with some sleep."

"I thought . . . ," Cindy began, ". . . I don't know."

"Hush, go to sleep," Harper said. "Say your prayers."

Sleep was so near to extinction, Cindy would have no trouble sleeping.

Harper seemed to grope for something more reassuring, failed, and turned reluctantly to the tape recorder. "Retrograde amnesia seems to be diminishing. The next interview should show real progress. End of Tape CRC 3." For a moment he gazed down at his patient with tired eyes. She seemed too small and frail to have survived so much. And what next? God knows. Perhaps he should try praying, too. Perhaps they all should.

3

During the two years her father had been posted to Saudi Arabia, Cindy had spent only part of one summer and one Christmas vacation there. Even if the government had been more stable, it simply wasn't a very productive place for a teenage American girl, but in December of 1987, with most of the world's nearly two hundred governments moving to the left or right, and few of them ever changing leadership by the elective process, Saudi Arabia seemed as politically healthy as most. More important, her father had not said no to the hint she'd dropped in a letter, and she refused to consider the possibility that he had not had time. Of course the check from her grandmother was a clear indication that Massachusetts was indicated, and she had reluctantly filled out a slip at the administration office to that effect. Perhaps if it had not snowed, or if the flu outbreak had not closed Le Rosey early, she would never have turned what began as a lark and a self-dare into a delightful but worrisome reality: the purchase of a Geneva-Beirut-Riyadh ticket, with sufficient money left over for a new tennis racket. Having done it, she felt a pang of guilt. Gram was getting on and Cindy loved her grandparents, but there were lots of other grandchildren home for the holidays. Worse was the fear of being forbidden, which could only come in the form of a call from her father that night at the dorm.

Packing with criminal haste, Cindy trudged across the campus within an hour of having bought the ticket. Some lower-schoolers pelted her with snowballs, which she fended off with the new racket. No one else saw her go or board the noon local to Geneva. With the train in motion she began taking stock: money adequate for a modest hotel and a cab, the ticket, a moment of panic as she groped for the black diplomatic passport. Idly she turned its pages as her heart returned to a more normal beat. "NAME: Cynthia Randall Cooper. BIRTH DATE: Sept. 20, 1971," which made her sixteen, a natural age to be, it seemed to Cindy. People of other ages were ranked in orderly fashion in front and behind, forming a harmonious setting for the sixteen year olds of this world, old enough no longer to consider themselves children, young enough to give older men wishful thoughts and to intimidate older women, sometimes. "BIRTHPLACE: Massachusetts, U.S.A. HEIGHT: 5 feet 2 inches," a bit too short. Still, Cindy repudiated high heels. She preferred jogging shoes and with her erect carriage she resembled a drum majorette. In action she was athletic, never tiring. She jogged laughing. In rare moments of repose she looked disturbingly mature. "HAIR: Blonde. EYES: Blue." Hair and eyes came from her father, along with the fine slim nose and the firm lips that marked the Coopers as old-family Boston. "DATE OF ISSUE: July 18, 1985," followed by, "THIS BEARER IS: A dependent of Howard B. Cooper, abroad on a diplomatic assignment for the Government of the United States of America."

The next page bore her photograph. That can't really be me, she thought. The eyes were so wide-open, looking shocked, as though in witness to some ghastly accident.

Though she had often drawn comments about fine bone structure, Cindy did not think of her face as delicate. The cheekbones were wide, the chin small, and the smile was open and boyish, suggesting she was more honest than she felt she was. A touch of flu or indigestion might have made that face look hollow-eyed, but healthy as she invariably was, and not suffering from unwarranted modesty, Cindy had to agree now that she was rather good looking.

Outside the steamy train window the lakefront scenery flashed by. The cubes and planes of the small clean towns, briefly framed and fusing with the lake blue, reminded her of Cezanne. When she returned from holiday, classes would have moved to the winter campus in the Bernese Oberland where the mountains were a constant presence, moving when you moved, brilliantly white in a blue sky that curved down to touch their peaks. This year she meant to be serious about skiing. But first, tennis, the Embassy pool, a tan. Cindy wanted to try everything, to be really alive. If the train were not rattling along she might have danced in the aisle. Instead she closed her eyes in pure contentment, opening them again as the train slowed into Geneva's northern suburbs.

From the station Cindy hiked down Rue du Mont-Blanc to the lakeside, forgetting that the Jet d'Eau with its four-hundred-foot stream of water was shut down for the winter. Worse, a darkening sky obscured the mountains. "Don't you dare," she warned the heavens. The Festival of the Escalade was going on in memory of the city's defense against the Duke of Savoy. Determined to derive some tourist benefit from the rapidly darkening day, she watched the costume parade and bonfire in St. Pierre Square. Before she gave up, a few flakes were drifting down, sufficient to powder her head and shoulders by the time she checked into the run-down Hôtel Angleterre, where she had supper alone, looking out on the dark lake into which the snow fell with silent perseverance. It was becoming the sort of night made to order for one who wishes to hold the weather responsible for anything that might happen.

Lying in bed that night she did not pray for the snow to go away, she willed it so, and as was often the case by morning the snow had obligingly stopped. A gray sky had settled comfortably onto the rooftops. Cindy paid the bill, the equivalent in francs of $180 with two meals, which left her $25 for the cab, barely enough with tip. The driver advised her in French that she would be wasting her time at the airport. "Like you Americans say, it is socked in." "Don't worry," she told him, "I have to get out of here. It will be all right."

At first the driver seemed vindicated. Nothing was landing, and all departures were indefinitely postponed. Cindy greeted a few homebound schoolmates in the crowded departure lounge. Finally came a report that the runways were cleared. "That's more like it," she said to herself, and at the last moment sent cables to her parents and grandparents. As she hurried to the boarding gate, she kept touching her purse to make sure that her ticket and passport were safe. Inside the plane, music rose gently from overhead speakers. She'd chosen a window seat near the back. Cindy had opened an Agatha Christie to page one when a not entirely unfamiliar voice full of Locust Valley, NY, exclaimed loudly, "Unreal. If it isn't the tennis wiz. How very nice to see you."

"It's nice to be seen," Cindy exclaimed, rather taken off guard. She recognized a senior from Le Rosey, Kim something-or-other, tall, slim, quite handsome, in a blue Brooks Brothers blazer with brass regimental buttons, khakis, and well-worn Sperry Topsiders.

"Mind if I plunk my stuff here?"

The plane was almost empty.

"Why not?" she replied, thinking, I'd like to get to know you, too.

"I hear your dad's a really awesome ambassador," he said.

"Oh, yes, uh, I mean, thank you." Cindy was still a bit flustered.

"Say, I don't think you know who I am."

"You're Kim, aren't you?"

"Kimball Anderson the third, actually. My dad's the new defense attaché at your dad's embassy."

"You're kidding."

The airplane began to taxi out into the thinning flakes. Red sunlight streamed into the cabin as the jet revolved in a slow arc and presently leaped forward as though given a sudden injection. Lake Geneva flashed briefly, was buried in cloud. The sky above opened and closed, a play of blue, gray, white, rippled by shafts of gold and silver, a wild fantasy of light playing on the mountains. Up safely, there was a general settling down and plumping of pillows. Ears grew accustomed to the hum of engines while far below the Alps gleamed with variegated color, their parapets thrusting above the storm clouds.

It didn't take Cindy long to decide that Kim was a good traveling companion, a bit old-style preppy, but so was she. While she'd done a term at Choate-Rosemary Hall, he'd been two years at Lawrenceville. They'd both summered in the Hamptons. He'd trashed a brand-new Audi there and seemed proud of it. While Kim had crewed on an Etchels out of Three Mile Harbor, she had preferred horseback riding, but they had both spent plenty of time sunning on Georgica Beach and even played tennis on the same courts, yet never met. "Well, this has to be fate," Kim said, and they felt like old friends. Apart from the reddish tinge to his hair—red hair, Cindy'd always heard, was angry hair—the only thing about Kim that disturbed her at first was the condition of his fingernails, bitten back to the quick.

"We may be in for an intense time," Kim said. "History in the making, with Saudi oil going for sixty bucks a barrel and the King's health failing, and all."

"Really? I hadn't heard about that."

"No? Well, I have it on good authority," he went on, adding, "The world's in a hell of a mess. I'm supposed to be off to Princeton in the fall, but I expect to be drafted during the summer."

"What a bummer," Cindy commiserated.

"Oh, well, soldiering runs in the family. Andersons have been in every war since the Revolution. My dad was a hero in the last one."

"Who remembers the last war? We're all so busy planning the next one," Cindy said, but the name Kimball Anderson rang a bell.

"Dad loved every minute of it. I suppose that shocks you."

"Why should it?" Cindy replied, trying to sound less astonished than she was.

"Dad said he never felt so alive before or since. Of course, wars aren't what they used to be. About the only chance I've got is South Africa. I expect they could use a few good mercenaries against those apes from Zimbabwe and Somalia. Not that I'm prejudiced or anything."

"How do you feel about Japanese cameras?"

Kim looked puzzled, then grinned. "Give me a German Leica any day."

"Don't suppose you go in for Arab cooking."

"Lord, no, my bag's full of Big Macs. Listen," Kim said, "I'm not really such a warmonger and racial bigot as I sound. Honestly."

"I should hope not," she told him rather fiercely.

"Hear her," Kim said, and laughed with boyish abandon. His laugh had saved him in frequent awkward moments.

"Are your folks expecting you? I think I'm arriving as a bit of a surprise."

"Dad'll be at the airport," Kim replied.

"Your mom's not out there?"

"No."

"Divorced? Not that it's any of my business."

"I wish it were that."

"I'm sorry." Cindy put her hand on his. "I'm always asking too many questions. When did you lose her?"

"You make it sound like carelessness. Actually, she's not dead, just departed. One night she surprised everybody by coming to an embassy party el buffo."

"Completely naked?"

"Starkers. She had the idea she was invisible. When she didn't shake off that notion, plus a few others that I'd rather not mention, Dad had to put her away in the nuthatch."

"Don't say that."

"What else?" Kim said. "The loony bin? Listen, it's a very ritzy, expensive place. How about the cracker barrel?"

"I'm sorry for your father."

"Don't be. I don't think they were married very hard."

"And for you." Kim offered no glib response and Cindy added quickly, "I guess I've been lucky." Her parents had always seemed that splendid two-headed creature a marriage should be.

"Oh, hell, Dad's parent enough for me," Kim replied.

"He's absolutely outstanding. Look." He'd pulled a photo from his wallet showing a stern-faced man in uniform, hair close-cropped, cradling a sword. It was an old-fashioned pose more suited to a daguerreotype. "That sword came to my grandfather from General Patton. I expect you've heard of him?" Cindy nodded. She'd made the connection. The Anderson Steel Company and its soldier sons. Old family, fabulously rich in a tremendously respectable and all-American way. "Patton was a gallant soldier, too." Then Cindy had to smile. Could one be gallant in modern warfare? The word seemed as archaic as the pose.

"What did your father do—in Vietnam, was it?" Cindy obliged.

The image Kim presented was of a dashingly destructive Boy Scout, exploding bridges, parachuting in off-beat uniforms behind enemy lines. "One of his wildest ideas was breaking up Buddhist riots with itching powder. Those monks didn't wear anything under their long robes, and the itching powder, well, it worked like a charm."

"Sounds sort of CIA-ish," Cindy remarked.

"It's not for me to comment," Kim answered with a half-wink.

By now they flew above the Adriatic, blue and throbbing with light, more fire than water. A green island swam serenely beneath and then behind them.

Presently lunch was served. Cindy chose lemon chicken, Kim, the shish kebob. "Not too gross," Cindy observed, starting on a slightly slimy wing. "Très déclassé," was Kim's reply. She talked him out of sending it back.

"You're not exactly psyched for rocking the boat, are you?" he said.

"I guess not."

"Maybe it's the soldier in me, always spoiling for a fight. Really, what do you mean to be when you grow up, so to speak? Tennis pro?"

"I happen to be mad for art," Cindy told him.

"Art who? Oh, you mean you're an artist? Paint, that sort of thing?" Cindy nodded. "I can't see you as the Greenwich Village type, somehow. Are you planning on growing a beard? Maybe you're just passing through a phase. I mean, hasn't all the paint that can be daubed on canvas been daubed already?"

"Listen, you philistine, don't spread it around but in fifty years the Met'll be paying a million bucks for an original Cooper."

"Maybe so. Mom paints her fool head off in the asylum. Paints the tables, paints the walls, the floor, herself, you name it. Seriously, how can anyone as pretty as you stand a chance? If you ask me, the art of love's more in your line than the love of art."

"Clever, clever, but just you wait. I have this feeling . . . it's hard to explain."

"Like maybe, somehow, you're elect?"

"Elect?"

"Yes," Kim said, "as if you've been chosen for some important purpose. I know I feel that way."

"How curious," Cindy said. It was too silly to repeat, but she remembered how once as a little girl she'd heard in half-sleep what she took to be Gabriel's trumpet calling her to some special task. Sitting up with the dawn light in her eyes and finding that a fire engine had supplanted the archangel, her disappointment was minor. There was plenty of time. The trumpet had not sounded again in her dreams, but she had never abandoned the notion that she was somehow special, on earth for a singular purpose, not merely for growing up, having a career, getting married, making babies. Perhaps it was art, but she didn't feel that sure of her talent. Still the conviction lingered and she might have mentioned it to Kim had not the plane, without warning, dropped several hundred feet. Plastic trays and plates, chicken parts, shish kebob bedded in yellow rice all rose and fell. A stewardess sat down hard in the aisle. Cindy scrunched back in the seat, digging her fingers into the armrests. As suddenly as it had begun the turbulence ended. "Outrageous!" exclaimed Kim, grinning. He might have been on a roller coaster. The pilot announced that the turbulence had been caused by hot air currents from the desert.

Formerly Swissair had routed through Cairo, but now, since the military takeover in Egypt and the subsequent rumors of a last Jihad against Israel, they touched down at Beirut International Airport. A handful of passengers got off. Fewer passengers boarded, mainly men with briefcases, bound, Cindy supposed, for the oil fields. The plane was nearly empty.

"I don't like it," Kim said. "I wish there were loads of passengers, even unwashed pilgrims on their way to Mecca. You know what they say about an empty plane in the Middle East being a sure sign of trouble."

Presently they were looking down on the Arabian peninsula through a cloudless sky. Kim hauled out a paperback copy of Doughty's *Travels in Arabia Deserta.* "You might want to borrow this," he said. "Over a hundred years out of date, but still relevant."

Cindy scarcely heard him. She was enthralled by the awesome empty expanse of sand and flint where men died for uncomplicated reasons: heat, cold, thirst, hunger. Even from such an air-conditioned distance it was terrifying, and yet somehow she felt drawn to it.

"You know," Kim went on, "they say that one day, when all the fertile soil and all the moisture in the rest of the world has been used up and polluted, life will make its last stand in the desert. Lord, what a place. How'd you like to cross it on a camel?"

"Like Lawrence of Arabia? Why not? I'm psyched."

"Of course the camels must all be gone," Kim added.

"Oh, no, there must be a few left." What was it about camels? As a kid you were supposed to have dolls and teddy bears. She'd had a Stieff camel named Binky, and she'd always collected them in glass and china.

"Look!" Kim interrupted. "There's a plane after us, a fighter."

"Two, no, four," Cindy said. She was next to the window and had the better view. The jet fighters seemed to be in random pursuit, not four abreast or in any other geometric formation, only four planes trying not to bump into one another.

"If it's some sort of escort, we'll be coming in soon," Kim said. But why an escort? An escort generally implied protection. Protection from what? A few moments later the no-smoking sign was lit and the Swissair jet settled too steeply for comfort, as if diving for cover toward the desert airfield outside of Riyadh. The fighters followed it down until Cindy could see their shadows cutting across the ground like dark scythes. Then they peeled away. She had a distant glimpse of the glassy office towers of Riyadh blinking under the brassy desert sun. Then they were down.

4

So silent, only the faint hum of electric generators. Cindy felt the pulse beat in her temple. She seemed to be swimming underwater toward cold pulsing light.

"Wake up, Cindy. Atta girl. You're doing fine. How are you feeling this evening?" Doctor Harper inquired. "You're looking much better. I bet you make the boys at Le Rosey nervous." Under the fluorescent panel he moved about like a ghost, without any shadow. Cindy noted that he was slightly stooped, as though he had spent too much time in the presence of supine patients. His voice had a calm and healing quality.

"I think I'm ready to go home," she said.

"That's good news," he replied. "Why don't you try sitting up, for a start?"

Cindy made it with an effort, her head spinning, perspiration beading her forehead and upper lip. She couldn't have held out long had not the doctor pressed a button that raised the head of the bed with a steady whine until it supported her shoulders. Cindy lay back gratefully against the pillow. "Oh, God." She felt so weak and nauseated. Despairing, she stared at the ceiling. From beyond the walls the hospital emitted an odd, mechanically digestive sound. She felt a slight tremor.

"Is this a ship?" she asked. "Are we on some sort of ship?"

"That's very perceptive, Cindy," the doctor said. "As a matter of fact, we are on a ship."

"Anchored?"

"In a way."

"Would it be possible for me to call my parents?"

"Maybe tomorrow."

"Just so they won't worry."

"Let's discuss it tomorrow. Now, how about something bland to eat, Cindy. Some soup? It will do you good," the doctor said, leaning toward her confidingly and pressing the rhetorical question, "don't you agree?"

"I'll try." Cindy dutifully took a few sips but the effort of sitting up made her stomach refuse.

"That's very good for a first try," Doctor Harper assured her. "Perhaps now we might talk a little, see what we can remember." Cindy shook her head in the negative. "Really, if you can't remember anything, what makes you think you're ready to go home?"

"Doctor . . ." Cindy was having trouble keeping the soup down. ". . . what's happened to me? Why can't I remember?"

"In simple terms, Cindy, you've had a concussion. You know what that is. It can blank anyone out for a while. We call it posttraumatic amnesia." He spoke with the calm precision of one who has learned a language thoroughly, not as a child but as an adult. "You've been aboard only twenty-four hours. It will all come back soon. Trust me, Cindy."

"I have a feeling I can trust you. You're like my father, kind of."

"I hope so," Harper said, looking down at his hands. He'd been trusted before and been found wanting. "But I can only ask the questions, Cindy. The answers have to come from you. Now, for the record, can you give it the old college try?" Cindy bobbed her head quickly in small affirmative nods as if she feared to speak the first word. "Good girl, but I don't want you moving your head too much. Just lie back and relax." He flipped on the tape recorder and with that metallic click one thought leaped out of Cindy's terrified confusion, and that was danger. Her recent memory was Pandora's box, still firmly sealed. Was it not wiser, certainly less painful, to leave it that way? Yet if she expected to go home, clearly it had to be faced.

"Let's pick it up from your arrival in Saudi Arabia," Doctor Harper was saying. "Apart from the fighter escort, did anything unusual happen at the Riyadh airport? Try to visualize it, Cindy. Let the thoughts flow, one at a time."

The whine of jet engines subsided and presently Cindy was blinking into the raging sunlight of Saudi Arabia. It felt good, but it stung her eyes, too. Except for the green flag with the white sword and Arabic lettering, the attendants in long white gowns, they might have landed at some obscure west Texas airport, an enormous one. The day was not hot but the terminal was frigidly air-conditioned and full of soldiers and police, the latter distinguishable only by their red berets. Several carried automatic weapons. This would have disturbed her at any time, but today was Friday, the Moslem sabbath, when Saudi Arabia supposedly devoted itself exclusively to God.

While a wizened little man with a three-day beard thumbed through her papers, Cindy noticed soldiers unloading what appeared to be sandbags from a truck. Still, Immigration nodded her along as though nothing were going on. The Islamic day began at sunset rather than midnight, and she reset her watch while a custom's official ticked off her luggage with a piece of chalk. No questions.

Passing through the security gate, Cindy found herself grinning and waving. Glimpsed through the crowd, her mother looked stunning. Clad in a plain white dress without ornamentation, she resembled a statue representing purity. Marjory Cooper had come from Burlington, Vermont, and with her chiseled face and alluring expression, had become a successful model in New York. Married, she had seemed the ideal diplomat's wife, charming, tastefully flirtatious, good at names, fashionably turned out. Embassy gossips swore that she had to be older than she looked. The one personal uncertainty Cindy had ever noticed in her mother was the dyeing of the first gray hairs. She was prepared as usual to tell Marjory how splendid she looked, but as they ran to greet each other she realized that her mother did not look well at all. Her face was puffy, the eyes darkly shadowed, sad as Pierrot.

Otherwise, Marjory seemed her usual self. She held out long arms driftingly as they embraced, then stepped back. "Turn around," she insisted, "all the way. Cindy, you look lovely."

"You look just great too, Mom," Cindy managed without much conviction.

"Liar, diplomatic liar," her mother said. "Nobody looks great for long in this frightful climate. And how are we to drag that great sack of yours? There simply aren't any porters."

"It's Friday, Mom."

"There are always porters," her mother insisted. "Something very peculiar is going on here."

"Don't worry, Mom, I can manage."

"I won't, but honestly, dear, if you ever gave us advance warning . . . We only just got your cable an hour ago. Your

father's out dedicating a new library and all the official cars are tied up there."

"You're not here alone?" Cindy asked, for she knew women were still denied driving licenses.

"No, fortunately I found someone. If I hadn't, what, may I ask, would you have done, dear? Hitchhiked, I suppose?"

"Mom, as a matter of fact I had things all worked out. I met this guy on the plane . . . over there. He's just come through the gate."

"With Colonel Anderson?"

"Right, that's his father," Cindy said, remembering the photograph. She waved from tiptoe and Kim waved back.

"Anderson has a son?" Marjory said with surprise. "I didn't even know he'd been married."

Kim and an older man strode toward them across the enormous lobby as though there was nothing but empty space in the way. The senior Anderson seemed alert for resistance. He carried his hands out from his sides, and robed figures made way as though he projected something as palpable as an electromagnetic field. Greetings were effusive. They might have been old schoolmates back for reunions, with Kim's father grinning throughout like a grand piano. Yet it seemed to Cindy that his eyes were coldly analytical, with nothing there but calculation and assessment. "I'm sure we'll see you lovely ladies later at the Embassy," he said, a signal that he wanted to depart.

Kim offered to carry Cindy's bag but their cars were in opposite directions and she shrugged it off with, "I'm lots tougher than I look."

"A pleasure meeting you, Mrs. Cooper," Kim said, and to Cindy, "Remember, we've got a match coming up. Center court."

"I presume that means he has a wife somewhere," Marjory said as they took the escalator down.

"Yes," Cindy said, surprised at all this speculation. "She's insane, at least that's what Kim said."

"Well, he seems like a very pleasant young man, but that father of his . . . I expect he's the only man in the world with clenched hair."

"Kim gave me the feeling he was in the CIA," Cindy said. Her mother shrugged. "Could he still be?"

"No, I'm sure your father would know a thing like that. Not that he'd tell me. You know how an embassy is, such rumors. If they were all true, that man would be a liquor smuggler, a white slaver, and the seducer of half the wives and all the secretaries in the compound, not that you can believe one thing you hear at those dreary cocktail parties."

Marjory talked and talked until Cindy realized it was her way of holding the alien world at bay, of denying the shrouded figures that watched them pass with the deathlike indifference of so many corpses. Their eyes revealed neither envy, curiosity, nor hate, only an enigmatic watchfulness like a collection of Goya's cats. When her mother said they would have to veil themselves for the drive into the city Cindy's "You're kidding!" was brief. She yearned just then to be private, anonymous, to be able to look out at the world but to remain unseen.

Still, she wondered why. "I think I told you I couldn't round up any of the limos with their lovely dark window glass. Mustn't offend the natives by riding around naked, you know, especially when they're having rather a traditional revival. Not that it won't blow over the way they have before, but if you'd consulted your father, Cindy, I don't believe . . . Well, you're here." She did not remonstrate. "Fortunately, at the last minute I ran into that young trans-

lator, you must remember him, Salim something-or-other?"

"Very well," Cindy said. "Salim bin-Kabina. I sometimes send him postage stamps for his collection."

"I know," Marjory said, "and I'm not sure I approve."

"Oh, Mother, really."

"Well, anyway, he drove me out. Over there, there's the car. But don't encourage him. The way these Bedouins drive . . . I don't mind the idea of dying instantly, but all sorts of broken bones . . ."

Salim had seen them and came for Cindy's luggage. He had the classic hawklike profile of the desert tribes, all sharply cut features with liquid dark eyes. "Good ee-wennin, Miss Cynthia," he said, and she was again enchanted by the way he pronounced her name. They shook hands, his long delicate fingers typically limp in the Arab way. His manner was shy, his voice had a cough lingering behind it. "You had a good trip, thanks be to God?"

"Very good," she said as he stowed the luggage in the trunk, "with a fighter escort to see us down, imagine that." Salim glanced at her with odd intensity. "Well, they didn't shoot at us." He held the door open deferentially. "Thank you," Cindy said, thinking that he really was quite exotic, like a breeze off the desert.

"I'm not used to traveling incognito," her mother said as they started up. "It's rather exciting." As they pulled away from the curb another car fell in behind them, a black limousine with square and imposing lines, driven by a chauffeur in a dark uniform with a visored cap.

Salim drove vigorously, treating the car as he might an unbroken steed. Still the limousine kept pace as they sped toward Riyadh. Flat, straight, and featureless at first, the road might have been the one to creation but for the six lanes of whizzing traffic, diesel trucks and buses for the most part. No fine horses, no camel caravans. The only thing to remind her of the Arabian Nights was a turbaned beggar.

"He'll never collect anything out here," she remarked.

"Oh, yes, Miss Cynthia," Salim assured her, swiveling half round as if the car was capable of directing itself. "That is a very good place for him. You see, the people call this the Highway of Death, because of the many accidents, you understand, and to give to that one is to receive luck against accidents."

"Wouldn't it be easier to drive more slowly?" Marjory interjected pointedly. She sat so straight that if only her upper half were visible Cindy might have thought she was mounted on a show horse.

"Ah, perhaps," Salim replied. "That is your Western thinking." He pressed the accelerator to the floor, swerving around a taxicab. "This is the East, and we have our own ways."

They hurtled on through palm and date groves where the older houses of mud brick and palm frond were giving way to cement and galvanized steel.

"You will be at the Embassy in no time, God willing," Salim assured them as he wrenched the steering wheel to avoid a small boy, his robe tied up around his waist, who wobbled out from the highway's shoulder on an oversized bicycle.

"You'd do very well at Le Mans," Cindy told him, enjoying the excitement. Salim grinned back in silent agreement. No question that he had a deft touch with a car, but he was wrong about the quick trip. Outside the city limits, traffic was being stopped by the Bedouin National Guard, a sinister crowd in Cindy's opinion, with their black headbands matched by black beards and mustaches. Salim put up an argument at the roadblock, stressing the prestigious nature of his cargo, to no avail. For reasons unexplained, all traffic was diverted onto a side road of packed dirt. A few slow-moving donkeys mingled with the vehicles, which hopelessly blew musical horns.

Presently the first tin, cardboard, canvas-and-plastic tarpaulin suburbs appeared amid a litter of soft-drink cans and bottles and the occasional dusty clump of wild grass. Gradually the dwellings became older, of mud brick tossed together like a child-god's blocks. Despite an air of decay and abandonment, the place teemed with life. Shops were closed behind ragged awnings but the air smelled of smoke and cheap pastries and the ever-present aroma of cooking lamb. The spectral forms of darkly veiled women clustered at high windows to absorb the street life with unseen eyes. Young men glared from doorways at the strange procession of passing cars. Near Masjid al-Joma, the Friday Mosque, pedestrian traffic slowed them to a crawl. In the past Cindy had always been whisked down broad avenues to the Embassy. This was unreal, a kind of remote travelogue. She was noticing how the veil sucked in and out with her breath when a figure ran out from the old Shara Palace Hotel, blocking the road deliberately. Suddenly it was very personal and threatening. As if plugs had been ripped from her ears, menacing noises roared in, the crash of brakes and the man shrieking in Arabic from a dark orifice studded with yellow teeth. He hurled a Coke bottle at the car and missed. Then a green-turbaned religious policeman, who had been rapping on the shutters of the market stalls to make them close for prayer, darted out, pinning the man's arms behind him. Salim swerved to avoid the pair while apologizing over his shoulder. "It is just the people expressing themselves. They are very polite people, Misses, but they wish for self-determination."

"What was that man shouting?" Cindy asked.

"That the only party is the party of God, Miss Cynthia. Just a fanatic who wishes for no Western reforms. Pay no attention, please. It is nothing to do with you. I apologize for my people."

Marjory rocked forward, her pale hands clasped over her knees. "Please, Salim, will you look where you're going. As a favor."

"Allah willing, I am a good driver, Madam. Do not fear."

Despite his words and adroit driving they were not out of it yet. Cindy heard the furious roar of a gasoline fire spring up in the center of a vacant lot where trucks parked on market day. Then one robed figure broke from the crowd surrounding the fire, cradling an oil can that exploded into a sheet of flame as he ran. There came a scream from the conflagration, as sudden and chilling as the flash of a strobe. Then dozens of people boiled into the street, their white robes like balloons in a tempest. They ran after the car, shouting and gesturing, but it was the pounding of those sandled feet that Cindy would remember.

Salim depressed the brake, mistaking it for the clutch. The big car bucked to a halt. Allowing the temperamental machinery no time to refuse, Salim forced the shift home, slewed the car around a concrete circle, horn blasting. Still it was not his alacrity that saved them but the fact that the mob had turned on the following limousine and were rocking it to and fro.

Abruptly the old quarter gave way. The car sped onto a broad avenue and the sky opened wide. Cindy took a deep breath, as though finally surfacing from deep and murky waters. Marjory lay back against the seat, her hands pressing the black veil to the contours of her face.

"Mom, are you okay?" Cindy asked her.

"Yes, yes, I'm quite indestructible," Marjory replied, and then pleadingly, "Would you light me a cigarette, dear? My hands seem to have gone all shivery." With the veil drawn aside, she took a deep drag, saying, "I have never cared for this place, never, not from the very first day." Now it's coming, Cindy thought, and I can't do a thing about it. "In fact, I hate it here. When we were first posted, I used to say to myself, 'Think of something worse.' Now it is worse." She laughed without mirth. "I don't think I want too much, maybe a little house in a quiet New England town. We could be making Christmas cookies now, Cindy." Marjory took a deep tremulous breath, near tears. "Well, I know it never will happen. I guess I'm still just a small-town girl without the thick skin you need to get along in a foreign embassy." She squeezed Cindy's hand. "We weren't expecting you, but I'm selfish enough to be oh, so glad you've come."

Cindy put her arm reassuringly around her mother's shoulder. It was an unaccustomed role and made her feel uneasy. Everything else that had happened simply seemed too weird to be true. It hadn't touched her at all, not like her mother's vulnerability.

They crossed the University campus, all concrete, glass, and sand, swung round the Royal Zoo, said to have the largest air-conditioning system in the world, and onto the avenue of the Ministries, palm trees and five-storied cement cubes. All quiet.

Salim drove very slowly now as though to compensate his passengers. "Permit me to apologize," he said. "I am not always so reckless a driver."

"We're not complaining. You did an outstanding job, didn't he, Mom?" Cindy insisted. "Didn't he, Mom?"

"Oh, yes, outstanding." Marjory sounded exhausted, ready to agree to anything.

"You see," Salim continued, "it gets worse late in the day, so I hurried. If it had not been for the detour . . ."

"You couldn't help that," Cindy protested.

"Thank you," Salim replied. "I'm not a wild Bedouin at the wheel. Please do not think that. From here there is no problem."

Outside the Qasr ar-Riyaasa Palace, guards in brown cloaks with golden-sheathed scimitars in their belts stood at attention. They looked bored. A huge neon Coca-Cola bottle winked on and off against the reddening sky. They hesitated at a pedestrian crosswalk marked with a headless human figure that Cindy found disturbing though she knew it was designed to placate Moslem zealots. Another block, another headless sign, and they pulled up before the gates of the United States Embassy where the Marine guards, resplendent in red, white, and blue uniforms, swung open the gates and saluted as they drove into the compound. For Cindy the place was a cross between a childhood memory of a palace and an Egyptian tomb, a sort of gargantuan Moslem-gothic, the price paid for goodwill and a Saudi architect. But it was home for the holidays, a solid, well-protected island of the good old U.S. of A., and Cindy breathed a deep sigh of relief.

Marjory sat back and took a long drag on her cigarette. "Thank God," she murmured.

"I'd hoped Dad might be looking out for us," Cindy said, disappointed.

"He ought to be back by now," Marjory agreed. "You go on, dear. I'd like to just sit here and finish this cigarette and collect my nerves, if Salim can put up with me for a few minutes more."

He held the door open for Cindy, saying, "I will have the bags sent up, Miss Cynthia."

"Oh, I nearly forgot, Mr. bin-Kabina, I brought a Christmas present for you. All sorts of stamps from everybody in the dorm. I bet you thought I'd forgotten. Well, you only get them on one condition, and that's if you cut out this 'Miss Cynthia' stuff. I'm Cindy. Try that, just Cindy." Salim looked embarrassed but he finally echoed her pronunciation. "That sounds good. Well, I'll see you all later."

Cindy went ahead. Everything thus far had left her confused and apprehensive. If anyone could reassure her and explain things it was her father. Someone had once said that an ambassador was an honest man sent abroad to lie for his country. Cindy did not believe it of her father. There was an old-fashioned expression holding that certain people have a word, meaning simply that they feel honor bound to keep their promise. Cindy knew that her father tried to have a word throughout a career that went back to 1968 when he was third secretary to the American Legation in Saigon during the Vietnamese crisis. He was second secretary in Guatemala when the attempted coups of the seventies were occurring, not to mention the disastrous earthquake in 1975. As chargé d'affairs in Egypt he'd seen the Camp David accords falling apart, spent a tranquil spell as Ambassador to Norway in the mid-1980s, and now for two years had his first really personal challenge, Saudi Arabia. For as long as she'd been conscious of the diplomatic process, Cindy had known the button on her father's desk labeled "Panic Button—Do Not Push." Marjory had intended it as a passing joke, but her husband had kept it there, and in Cindy's mind he was the last person to resort to such a thing even if it were real. He'd always seemed so calm, so on top of any situation, though he'd once confided that it wasn't so. "An ambassador has to seem that way," he'd told her, "but if he's doing his job, he's like a swan, sweetheart, very elegant and dignified on the surface, but down in the murky water, believe me, he's paddling like mad."

Cindy had noticed the paddling only occasionally, like the time in Guatemala when the students demanded an American flag to burn. They'd begun throwing stones until her dad had gone outside, acting cool as a cucumber, though she knew he'd been scared from the way he'd been cracking his knuckles. In the interests of encouraging home exports, he'd told the students where they might purchase a flag. That was the story afterward. Whatever he'd really said, they'd gone peacefully away, leaving Cindy with the impression that there was nothing her father couldn't handle.

At the front desk she asked the receptionist where the Ambassador was. "Sorry, Miss Cooper," he said after she'd identified herself, "we've all had a long day. Your father's at home in the Residence. Do you know where that is?" Cindy knew. The Embassy compound occupied some dozen acres with the Residence on the far side. If it weren't an embassy with its dignified air she might have run all the way. Figures in white pounded about the tennis courts. The pool winked at her invitingly but she hurried along. A Marine guard was posted near the front entrance but he recognized her and swung open the door.

She found her father in his private office, a tall, grave headmasterly-looking man with glasses that tended to slip down on his nose. She was around the piled desk before he could get to his feet. "Cindy, sweetheart," he said, hugging her, "are you early or am I late? If I'd known you were here . . ."

"Are you very angry with me, Dad?" Cindy asked for the record, knowing there was no need.

"When am I angry with you? How was the trip?"

"The plane was fine, Dad." Then she told him about the trouble in the streets. "What about that limo, Dad? Was that one of ours?"

"Let me check," he said. "I don't like the sound of it." He spoke rapidly into the telephone on his desk, listened solemnly, then replaced the receiver. "Afraid it was one of ours. They'll get back to me about what happened. I suppose your mom's all shaken up."

Cindy nodded.

"And she gets out so seldom, too," he said, as though he were to blame. "Not that it has anything to do with us directly."

"Is the King really so ill, Dad?"

"We get all kinds of conflicting reports, sweetheart. Don't let it prey on your mind." Years of diplomacy had made Howard Cooper something of an actor. His frowns and smiles seemed always the clothing for his last statement or the appropriate reaction to a remark made to him. Yet despite this characteristic Cindy always sensed her father had emotions, strong ones. "Only I wish you'd cleared this visit with me first."

"Then I wouldn't be here now, would I?"

"Not necessarily." Still, the answer would have been "no," she felt certain, "no" and made to like it, because it would have been a government order. Her father could tell a friend he had bad breath in such a way as to leave him feeling grateful and touched. "Let's chat in the garden before they turn on the electric eye or whatever it is out there." After dark, sensors attached to alarms would ring and Marine guards would come running.

The garden was already cool under the palms.

"Mom seems so hyper it scares me," Cindy said.

Her father nodded. "She needs a vacation. You'll do her no end of good."

"I hope I do. She worries so."

"She'd like to worry about crabgrass and worms in the poodle."

"What poodle?" Cindy asked, surprised.

"Exactly. What crabgrass? You know, sweetheart, I'll always be glad I married your mom, but I often wonder why she married anyone in the foreign service. She so hates the uprooted life."

"Especially here," Cindy agreed.

The air was sweet with jasmine and orange blossoms. A pale moon swam in the yellowing sky, seeming among the palm fronds as thin and worn as an ancient coin. The craters were the same hue as the sky so that Cindy had the impression she was gazing through to the cosmos beyond. Endless space. Still, in any direction other than up, her mother's world ended within a hundred yards: a comfortable, well-equipped prison, but a prison all the same.

"I guess I never counted on one thing," her father said.

"What's that?"

"Your ever growing up. It's a look you have."

"What kind of a look, Dad?"

"Of the woman you're going to be very soon."

"A good woman?"

"I think a much more than good woman. Something really special." He put an arm around her. "Come on, they'll be switching on the juice any minute. We ought to round up your mom and have something to eat. We're lucky it's Friday and there's nothing official on tonight."

It was like old times. Marjory Cooper had composed herself and Howard relaxed in a robe and the same shabby old slippers he'd shuffled around in evenings when Cindy was little enough to sit on his lap. He said they made him feel comfortable. Her mom called them his security slippers and had given up trying to find replacements. Funny that he needed such props. Cindy had endured so many meals in transit that she only snacked on some bread, cheese, and cold chicken.

The evening's one sour note was sounded when Marjory said, "You know, dear, I'm not sure it's wise being so familiar with the natives."

"You mean Salim? Oh, Mom."

Drawn in as reluctant arbiter, Howard said only, "He's a very competent young man, Marjory. I don't see the harm."

Further analysis was averted by the ringing of the telephone, which Marjory seized as though she meant to throttle it. "Yes, what is it?" she demanded. "I see." She handed it over to her husband who said only, "Cooper here," listening patiently, then concluding with, "and thank you, Colonel Anderson."

"Was that about the limo?" Cindy wanted to know.

"Yes. The car's a bit worse for wear, but our people are safe. I think it might be appropriate if we drank a toast in thanksgiving."

So Marjory produced a bottle of French champagne smuggled in via diplomatic pouch and Cindy, touching glasses with her parents, knew she was glad she had come. There was such a warm, loving atmosphere that evening, like a Renoir painting, she thought, her favorite artist who loved painting quiet happiness so much that he went right on after the brush had to be bound to his arthritic hand. Outside, dusty evening light fell on distant white minarets, turning them rose-colored, like blood-tipped spears thrusting into the sky.

Presently Cindy went to her room. It was anyone's guest

room, really; high-ceilinged with a long mirror and the bed-spread, chairs, and drapes all of the same deep blue fabric. From the window Cindy could only hear the city, strange and evocative, for her room overlooked the Embassy garden. Small birds fluttered in the palms. How peaceful it seemed, until from their high-pitched whickerings in the shadowy spaces she realized they were really bats. Then, with the sun sliding over the edge of the world, Cindy was aware of the end of light and warmth. The Embassy seemed to shed its sheltering walls and with the coming night she felt like a cave dweller guarding some high place among stones. A muezzin chanted the call to prayer in a voice of silver clarity, and that summons was magnified, echoed, and re-echoed by a hundred microphones throughout the city, a call that seemed to come from the heart of the people, encompassing the strength and suffering of its long history. "There is no God but God and Mohammed is his messenger . . ." Cindy shivered, feeling the cold that came with the abrupt dark. ". . . Prayer is better than sleep . . ." Already she missed the mountains and the long Alpine dusk. Here the desert swallowed up the sun instantly. A brief tension in the air, a flicker, and then it was night, with the people kneeling to pray.

She seemed to see those kneeling figures, the desert crowds bowed in reverence down through the ages. Faith in one God had come from the desert, where in that vast emptiness lonely men had contemplated the oneness and majestic order of the universe. It had come in three great waves, Judaism, Christianity, and Islam, each acknowledging its predecessor but claiming a purer form of revelation, which still made for deadly antipathy. According to Cindy's Middle Eastern Studies class at Le Rosey, the Moslems called all that preceded Mohammed "The Time of Ignorance." With his coming in 622 A.D., Islam had borne his word east to India and west as far as Spain, and over the centuries defended with the sword their version of faith. In Arabia that sword had passed into Turkish hands, and cultural stagnation had set in until the mid-eighteenth century, when the Wahhabi revival of Islamic purity began. Not until 1902 did Ibn Saud carry the renewed faith over the walls of Riyadh, where he surprised the Turkish army garrison. Within ten years the Turks were driven out, and the new nation was named Saudi Arabia in honor of its founder. Ibn Saud's descendants ruled there still, princes of the royal house by the thousands. But now the desert had lost its isolation. The land was rich in oil beyond dreams of avarice. Prayer five times a day might heal the soul, but the body lusted after worldly goods. In that struggle's outcome lay the future of this desert land.

The muezzin's call, the onrushing desert cold, spoke for that backward-gazing soul. But the street mobs, the flaming petrol, were they not the angry voices of the material present? Cindy was too tired to think it out. She shivered, longing for sleep. Hastily she stripped off her clothes, arranged them neatly in the large closet, caught sight of her nakedness in the mirrored door. You'll do, she told herself. Within a modest frame she was well proportioned. Perhaps she would never acquire that quality described in *Cosmopolitan* as allure, or the full bosom for which she occasionally yearned, but she was well and athletically assembled. No, nothing to be ashamed of. Having pulled a nightgown over her head, Cindy returned to the window to fix a wish upon the first star. Too late. What sharp eyes the Wise Men must have had to see just one in all that whirling galaxy. She pressed her nose against the screen until the tip was molded into tiny dark squares. Above the gentle whine of mosquitoes she heard the faint rustling of the palms stirring in the desert breeze, and something else, not so much a sound as an intangible sense of intrusion. She knew someone was in the garden. Impossible, with the electronic sensors down there, and still as she went to bed she had the feeling of being watched until the room was dark.

"Allahu akbar—God is most great," echoed the muezzin's summons. "Prayer is better than sleep." But Cindy had come a long way that day, farther perhaps in time than in space, and if she could compose her racing mind it was sleep that she would have.

5

Doctor Harper had been called from the room. He'd left the tape recorder going and Cindy watched the twin drums slowly turning in silence. The needle and tube were gone from her arm, which must mean she was better, and better ought to mean going home. She could walk now. One of the two doors led to a small bathroom. She hazily recalled having a shower there. If this were an ordinary hospital the other door would lead home, but it wasn't. Still, to know what was outside might give her a clue, and she'd laid her hand on the knob when she heard Harper arguing with someone. He sounded vehement, and having prevailed, opened the door and closed it behind him with exaggerated care.

"Up and around," he said with evident surprise. "That's good to see."

"Was that about me?" she asked, not wanting to seem like an eavesdropper.

"Only very indirectly," Harper said. "Don't concern yourself, Cindy. How's the memory doing?"

"I wish you'd ask somebody else. There are lots of people much better informed than me."

"For instance?"

"Mom and Dad."

"I wish they were here, too," Doctor Harper replied.

"We aren't keeping you apart, believe me. You do believe me, Cindy?"

"I believe you," she said reluctantly, "but where are they?"

"I'd tell you if I knew," Harper replied.

"Can't I please talk to them over the phone? Or the ship's radio, or whatever?" Cindy could see another negative forming on Harper's lips and said hastily, ". . . or my grandparents. They must be terribly worried."

"I can confirm this for you, Cindy, but I'm sure they know where you are. I hate to be so persistent," he apologized. "You've had one hell of a time and I hate doing this. I don't suppose you believe me when I say it's for your own good as well."

"When I try to remember certain things I get so afraid I black out. There must be somebody else you can ask. Colonel Anderson. Speak to him."

"I would if I could," Harper admitted.

"You're saying that because he's dead, aren't you?" Cindy asked him very calmly. It wasn't deduction, or memory in the usual way, but something she suddenly knew without a doubt. The horror came only secondarily, as though a phantom hand had laid its cold touch upon her shoulder. She felt the touch but dared not look back for fear of what else she might see.

"I'm not in possession of many of the facts," Doctor Harper replied. "I'm hoping you are, if we can just find the key."

"I might do better if this weren't so mysterious," Cindy protested, "if I knew what was going on. I mean, my arm's all bandaged. Did I do that to myself? Doctor Harper, did I?"

He took both her hands in his, saying solemnly, "I don't think so. There's no reason to think so, Cindy. I firmly believe it was an accident. As far as I'm concerned, you're a remarkably stable young woman. To have been through . . . well, I can only imagine. These are all things with which you must come to grips. I'm here to help you. Please, we haven't much time. Trust me, Cindy."

"Time? I don't even know what time it is. Is it day or night?"

"It's 11 P.M., July the 27th. What can you tell me, Cindy, about that translator, Salim bin-Kabina? You did know him?"

"Did? Is he dead, too?"

"I meant it when I said I'm not in possession . . ."

"But Colonel Anderson is dead, isn't he?" Cindy interrupted. She seemed to see one of those pedestrian-crossing signs all splashed with blood. "They cut off his head and you know it."

With evident reluctance the doctor said, "To the best of my knowledge, yes, Anderson is dead. He has been dead for some time."

Cindy saw sun glinting on the blade of a raised sword, saw the blade slash down.

"Would you care to talk about it?" She gave no answer. "About Colonel Anderson being killed?" Danger. They were moving into danger. Cindy felt as if the metal walls of the small room were drawing closer. She breathed deeply through her mouth, her breath coming shorter and shorter, shallower and shallower. The oxygen seemed to be vanishing from the air.

"Do you feel all right, Cindy?" Doctor Harper asked. "Do you need a pill?"

"No. No, thank you."

"But you don't want to talk about Anderson."

A long silence.

"I can't," she said finally. "Doctor, am I having a nervous breakdown?"

"We don't use that expression anymore, Cindy. You've been under considerable stress, both mental and physical. Now let's talk about something more pleasant. Tell me how Christmas vacation went after you settled down in Riyadh."

"If I can remember," Cindy replied. Those days were like a narrowing tunnel through which she could not quite force her thoughts, but Christmas did not seem to threaten. She remembered a real pine tree, bright with ornaments and tinsel.

"Cindy, in our last session you told me about the first night at the Embassy and how you suspected that bin-Kabina was in the garden."

"Did I?" Again her memory blurred.

"Can you recall seeing any more of him before Christmas?"

"Just a silly fuss over tennis. It wasn't anything," she said, remembering her own anger and embarrassment.

At the American Embassy in Riyadh, tennis as a rule was played early or late, beginning before the raising of the flag that flew over the courts, ending sometimes after its ceremonial furling. The exception was winter days when the north wind blew from the desert, and even then, if it blew hard the air was so apt to be full of sand and dust that no one went outside unless it was necessary. Cindy and Kim had agreed on early, just after sunrise. Cindy went to meet him, ducking her head from the fierce sunshine. Kim was already on the court, practicing serves in his Lacoste whites. His hair was tastefully windblown as though he'd just returned from a successful sailboat race. They rallied briefly. Cindy, quick on her feet, seldom failed to return a ball. Kim pounded away, sometimes wildly, making the chain-link fence ring. He was red in the face after the first set, which Cindy took without straining.

"It's getting pretty hot," she said.

"Come on!"

"We're not used to this climate yet."

"Best two out of three," Kim demanded. Presently it was best three out of five.

Veins stood out on Kim's forehead. The pallor of his complexion changed to peony.

Cindy was a winner by nature but not an insistent one. She lacked sufficient passion and the absolute concentration to allow her to stand all day with eyes on nothing but the ball. Besides, she did not want Kim having a stroke, so she began easing up, letting the third set go 7–5, offering to concede the others. Nothing doing, Kim panted. He was out for blood, and lest he shed his via a coronary she let the match slide away.

Kim was delighted. "You're not bad," he said, leaving out the half-expected, "for a girl." "Of course, if I'd been on my game from the start . . ."

Walking back to the Residence they met Salim, also in tennis whites, racket in hand.

"May your day be prosperous," he said, the Arabic version of "good morning."

"I didn't know you played," Cindy remarked.

"Not very well at all, Miss Cindy, but I am meeting with my friend and we shall try this Western game of yours." Then, turning to Kim, "Young Mr. Anderson, yes?" Salim held out his hand.

Kim nodded a greeting. He did not trouble to shake hands, seeming not to notice that Salim had intended to do so. His attitude, his smile were Byronic, at once contemptuous and world-weary.

"This is nice," Cindy pressed on. "We ought to try doubles one day, shouldn't we, Kim?"

Kim's lips parted and a movement in his jaw told Cindy that his tongue was touching the roof of his mouth. Finally he said blandly, "As a rule, I only go in for singles."

"We are just beginning this tennis game," Salim observed with a faint smile.

"Yes, of course," Cindy rushed to say. "It takes a long time to get the knack. You and your friend must practice for ages."

"Yes," Kim agreed, sounding bored and enervated, and Cindy hoped that the language barrier would screen out the insincerity that was all too plain to her.

"You make fun," Salim said. "But one day, Mr. Anderson, we will surprise you."

"Yes, I'm sure you will. One day."

"Good-bye, Miss Cindy," Salim said.

"Salim, don't . . ." Cindy began, but the Arab had already turned.

Smiling, Kim kissed the tips of his fingers in adieu. Softly he jangled some coins in the pocket of his shorts.

"That wasn't very nice," Cindy turned on him, outraged. "Are you trying out for the ugly-American-of-the-year award, or what?"

"My, you are touchy. If you want to know, I didn't much like the way you were flirting with that character."

"Flirting! I was just trying to be pleasant."

"I saw the looks you were giving him. Listen, you don't flirt with a wog and get away scot free. One friendly wink and they think you want to be carried off to their harem. That's the way their minds work."

"How ridiculous."

"I kid you not," Kim said, beginning to laugh.

"Really hilarious. What's tickling your Stone Age sense of mirth now?"

"I've never seen you angry before. I suppose it has something to do with getting beaten . . ."

"Kim Anderson, you are the most cocky, the most pompous, the most chauvinistic . . . oh, I can't think of enough names to call you!"

"Admit it," Kim said. "You think I'm terrific."

"Leave us not be imbecilic." Cindy was really angry now. "I'd pick that 'wog,' as you call him, any day."

Kim laughed, a mechanical "ha, ha," but his face reddened. "Look, okay, I'm sorry. Calm down. I won't call him a wog. Let bygones be bygones . . . Cindy!"

She had begun walking away, her back rigid. "I'll think about it," she said, not turning around. Kim shook his head in disgust sufficient to restore his self-esteem and stalked off in the opposite direction.

For the gesture's sake, Cindy had taken the wrong path. Facing the tennis courts again, she noticed that Salim was alone there, apathetically bouncing a ball against the backstop. She might as easily have gone on, had a swim, but since he was alone she wanted to make up for Kim's behavior. Besides, Salim had seen her and smiled, a white gash of a smile in his dark face.

Always direct, Cindy said, "I want you to know I'm sorry about Kim Anderson. He was very rude."

"Please do not apologize, Miss Cindy."

"Hey, I'm just Cindy, remember?"

"He is perhaps your boyfriend, Cindy?" Salim had a fierce face, but the eyes were soft and circled by such a sad and gentle melancholy that it killed in her all emotion but sympathy.

"Kim? Oh, good grief, no! We just met on the plane

coming out here." Wanting to be generous, she added, "You have a fantastic command of English."

"Not really. One day, perhaps, yes. I am learning, but Turkish and Russian, those are—how do you say?—my proficiency."

"Really?" Cindy said, impressed. Thanks to Le Rosey she could manage in French, stammer a bit of German. "Not many people have such a gift for languages. I know I don't. Where did you pick it up?"

"Please?"

"Where did you learn English?" The conversation was sinking in quicksand, she thought, and her head had begun to pound from the sun.

"At the University of Riyadh," Salim replied, "and before that at the King's School, the high school. Very many of our instructors are from America, you know."

She really had to get out of the sun. "Are you coming to the Embassy Christmas party?" Cindy said, trying to break away and feeling suddenly embarrassed.

"Oh, no, the staff never attends, never in history."

"Well," she said, turning to leave, "I could give you all those stamps if you came. Oh, I'm not trying to convert you or anything. I'm not really into religion." She laughed and knew it sounded forced.

Salim reddened. "Things change here very rapidly, but not that rapidly. It would not be suitable."

"Sorry, sorry . . . I didn't mean . . ."

A ghost of a smile went to his high cheekbones but he did not answer. Without forethought she caught his hand, gave it a reassuring squeeze. He in turn simply held her hand, as if feeling its weight, then let it fall. Her embarrassment increased. You never knew where you were with these

Saudis. Did sharing hands with a woman somehow offend him?

"I've got to go in now," Cindy said, edging away, smiling at Salim to be polite and friendly, to make up for the ugly American. Salim smiled back with magnificent white teeth, and there was a quality Cindy had not expected, that of mischief. Still it was the sad dark eyes that made her tingle. She really had to get away.

Extrication came in the form of Salim's tennis partner, another young Arab embassy employee.

"My dear Cindy," Salim said, "when one is warm to me I am warm to him back. You are my friend now, and I shall never change, even if you do."

His look was so intense Cindy felt she might catch fire, the way dry leaves can be kindled by a magnifying glass. "Yes, me too," she hastily agreed, and after a brief introduction to the friend, who was a Palestinian in the car pool, she said, "See you later, and oh, Merry Christmas."

As she turned away, Salim had the impression she had winked at him. It put him off his game entirely, and for the first time he lost every set.

"You're doing very well," Doctor Harper said. "We've run out of tape again. Are you too tired to go on, Cindy?"

"I'm fine, really."

"How's the old head?"

"Pretty good."

"Can you go on a bit?"

"Yes," she said, "but I don't see how any of this is helping you, or me."

"We'll see," the doctor replied as he installed a new cassette, numbered CRC 5, in the machine. "Nothing else before Christmas that bothered you?"

"No, not really."

"Did you see bin-Kabina again?"

"Salim? No, not before Christmas. I felt like a fool, acting the way I did."

"No other incidents like the street business?"

"No."

"You must have had some inkling of what was going on behind the scenes."

"No. Well, yes, in a way. I mean, Dad did sort of fill me in. It was just before the Embassy Christmas Eve party."

"I think we could use that, for the record, Cindy."

"But he told me it was all confidential," she protested.

"Maybe then," Doctor Harper said, "but that was a long time ago. It can't hurt anyone now."

Cindy had very little chance to talk with her father in the days before Christmas. Though she never left the Embassy compound, there was a repressed air of heightened activity and tension upon which her imagination fed: official cars coming and going, endless meetings behind closed doors, and the murmur of crowds gathering in the city beyond the walls where little flares of hatred were erupting—a bomb at a gas station, a man shot down inside a coffee house, a car overturned and burned on the airport road—small flames of hate flickering in the dark but never strong enough to begin the conflagration. Then, on the afternoon of Christmas Eve, she'd found her father alone behind his desk, one hand on the phone, as motionless and dully staring as a waxworks' dummy.

"Dad, I've hardly seen you."

"I know it, sweetheart. It's been one damned thing after another. Come on, give the old man a hug." She gave him a back rub as well. "You're here at just the right time with those strong hands of yours. Lord knows I'm uptight."

"Everybody seems to be," Cindy said. "I wish I knew half of what's going on."

Howard Cooper was too honest a man to harbor something in his heart for long unless it was classified top secret. He liked to get things out in the open. "Come on," he said, "I'll show you something, something you asked about last time."

"Is this a guessing game, Dad?"

"No, honey, I'm talking about the inner sanctum, the glass room, if you really want to talk shop."

The Chancellery building faced the south side of the compound. It attempted in no way to compromise with Arabic taste but was one of those metallic glass cubes so popular in the American Southwest. Conference rooms and offices made up the above-ground floors. It was quiet now, except for the swish-thud of handbrooms wielded constantly by the cleaning men, for even in a sealed structure such as this the dusty wind made every day a cleaning day. The more sensitive rooms were in the basement, behind Marine guards and steel doors: the code room, the pouch room. "The file room," the Ambassador said, "contains enough material to indict the civilized world. At least we like people to think so, which is why we keep the door locked even if there's nothing behind it." For private conversation, a soundproof room was required, if possible a room within other rooms, and in this case a free-standing glass box large enough to contain ten easy chairs and a conference table.

"Welcome to the cerebral chamber," her father said. Cindy stood a moment in silence as though at the threshold of a forbidden zone.

"Awesome," she said, and stepped inside.

"Sound-proof, bullet-proof, all the comforts," Howard Cooper said. "No secrets are stolen from this place. If you wanted information from the American Ambassador, who would be your spy?"

"Me. I mean, why not his daughter?"

"Seriously."

"Your secretary."

"Not bad."

"Or your driver, maybe the switchboard operator."

"How about a translator?"

"Dad, do you mean Salim?" Cindy was startled. The game seemed to be losing its fun.

"Too suspicious. Besides, he sees no classified material. No, someone more all-American."

"Kim Anderson, a secret agent."

"That would be a good cover."

"Or his father," Cindy added.

"Your guess is as good as mine," her father replied.

"Then you think Colonel Anderson is a . . ."

"You said it, I didn't. Really, I have no idea," said the Ambassador.

"I thought he was in the CIA or something," Cindy said.

"I don't know. I don't think I care to go on record one way or the other where Anderson is concerned. He's a competent person, you understand, an awfully competent person. I'd be perfectly willing to say that, but he's a queer fish. Maybe it's the way he's always whistling Sousa marches, off key at that. I wish we didn't have to have places like this, but as long as we do, and we're here, what would you like to ask?"

"Well, I don't know." Cindy was overwhelmed with the

possibilities. "Everything. Is the King really dying? What happens if he dies?"

"Maybe nothing. The Saudis are a strong family, but that's not to say the lid won't blow off." The Ambassador sat forward as if, even sealed as they were in glass, they might be overheard. "Back in sixty-nine some officers attempted a coup. It hasn't been forgotten."

"I guess what I really want to know is, what could happen to us?" Cindy asked, her hands pressed together as though in pain. "I always thought they needed our help."

Saudi oil for U.S. technology and weapons. On the surface it was a fair exchange. "But there's a catch," her father explained. He walked around the glass room, touched the back of a chair, picked up a pad of paper from the table. He seemed to be weighing his words carefully and as she waited, Cindy noticed for the first time that her father was a bit hunched: a tall man, but just now like a tall bird drawn down by winter weather. "You see, the Saudis are selling their soul into the bargain. They're a proud, God-fearing people with a glorious past. Once, they nearly conquered the world, and now they can be thrashed by a little Western nation like Israel. To catch up, they must admit that the past is dead, that even their God may have lost out to our science. It makes for a humiliating situation, and there are many Saudis who hate us for it."

There was a difficult silence after he spoke. "It sounds depressing," was all Cindy could think of. She sat stiffly, her face as solemn as if asking questions in a court of law. "But Dad, I still don't know who is trying to do what to whom."

"Fair enough," her father replied. He enjoyed diagraming situations elaborately and began producing ballpoint pens from his jacket pockets, finally finding one that wrote. "Now, here we have the King, around him his relatives. As far as we're concerned, they're trying to peacefully reconcile the past and the present. Now surrounding them are the royal National Guard, made up of old desert tribes and loyal to the death. No problems so far."

"So who do you put on the other side of the pad?" Cindy wanted to know.

Her father looked up, smiling. "Sweetheart, you have just asked the jackpot question. The Saudis tend to blame their problems on Jewish communist subversives. That's a handy label for breaking up strikes among the oil field workers. A bigger problem is an aversion to physical toil. I'm not talking about laziness, but a religious conviction that manual labor is demeaning. Until recently, women have been forbidden to work at all. There goes half the work force."

"But all that's changing," Cindy interrupted.

"Very slowly. And the men, if they have any say, will only take executive jobs, so who does the dirty work?"

"Foreign labor." She wasn't entirely ignorant.

"Palestinian refugees and Yemenites for the most part, a lot of Pakistanis, and most of this crowd wouldn't mind a bit if some army officer threw the royal family out and created a so-called socialist republic, as Nasser did years ago in Egypt."

"Will they, Dad?"

The Ambassador pinched the bridge of his nose, grappled for the right words. "It depends on whom you ask. Talk to General Aziz—he'll be here tonight, by the way—and he'll tell you the army's loyal to a man. Others, including myself, are not so confident. Officially, there's no subversive movement afoot. Unofficially, it's a bit of a headache. If it gets rolling, the next stop is civil war. No more oil being shipped out, so we get involved. Besides, with an election year coming up, the President can't afford to be called soft. And away we go."

"Is it that bad?"

Her father raised his eyes slowly with the polite attention of a gentleman whom nothing can surprise. "Not 'is it,' but 'can it get.' Yes, sweetheart, it might get that bad. The world's a tinderbox right now. India's talking about attacking Burma for rice. The Soviet economy's in trouble, and Poland is acting up again. Lord knows how long that army clique can keep the lid on Iran." Then he sighed and said, "Oh, Cindy, I don't like any of it." He dug the tip of the pen into the pad, making a red hole with its tip that he gradually widened. "What do the Soviets do if we use force to protect the oil flow from the Middle East? And we would. It's a dangerous thing to drive one's enemy to despair. It makes him strong."

"So you think there'll be war."

"Maybe I'm an optimist, but let's say I feel there won't be. It's only a gut thing with me, but it seems as if you have to take the world's blood pressure, in a way, sense its mood. War requires a kind of world permission. I don't think we have it, not yet."

"You're scaring me, Dad."

"Forgive me. I'm making it sound more threatening than it is. It won't come to that, I promise. There are rational men on all sides in this business. No more wars." He sounded so eager to reassure and yet so overwhelmed by doubts. "The main thing is, and don't let this upset you either, the Embassy may presently go on alert status. That only means the staff remains constantly available by phone. Mustn't precipitate a crisis by overreaction."

"How does that affect me?" Cindy asked with growing apprehension.

"It means, I have to be honest with you . . ."

"When you start like that I know something disagreeable's coming," she interrupted.

"It only means that one of our Air Force jets is standing by, in the event an evacuation of staff dependents seems advisable. I doubt it will come to that, but I want you and your mother prepared. Actually, she'd welcome a vacation. I hope things will level off, and yet there is something in the air," he added in his calm, academic voice, "which makes me wonder."

"I'll keep my bags packed," Cindy promised gloomily.

"You needn't go that far. I want us to have a merry Christmas, if we live through the party tonight and General Aziz. There's a man I can't fathom. He'll play the clown, more than likely, but you mustn't underrate him. Well, as Henry the Fifth was wont to say, once more into the breach, dear friends. I may have said this before, but it's good having you here, kiddo," and he tugged Cindy into his arms. She rocked against him, rubbed her cheek on his shirt. "I know I don't have to caution you not to worry your mom with what we've discussed. You won't, will you, sweetheart?"

"I won't tell a soul, Dad," Cindy promised, nor did she until she spoke to Doctor Harper with the tape recorder going.

6

"Cindy," said Doctor Harper, "I take it you attended the Christmas Eve party."

"Yes, of course."

"And your recollection is clear?"

"I think so."

"Did you meet General Aziz at the party?" Cindy nodded. "How did he seem?"

"Very jolly, as though he'd been drinking."

"Liquor?" asked the doctor.

"Of course he hadn't been, but he was so different."

"Different?"

"From later on," she replied.

"Tell me whatever you can remember about that evening, if you think you're not too tired."

The immense reception room, cool on the hottest days, with an air of solitude, seemed almost like home that evening. There was holly and ivy on the big marble mantle, holly and ivy and red ribbon twined round the chandeliers—plastic, of course, but nice if you didn't get too close or try to smell. The tree was real. Cindy, her mother, and Kim Anderson did the final decorating. Marjory Cooper had preserved a fragile gaiety. When Kim accidentally dropped a bulb she gasped as though a thorn had run under her thumbnail. The Marine guards at the end of the room snapped their guns to attention; then they all laughed with relief, even the guards. Cindy could not deny the tension but she was determined to ignore it and have a good time. One simply had to at Christmas. Of the three, only Kim seemed to require no conscious effort. His blue eyes were bright. He looked scrubbed and clean all through.

"What are you giving your mom for Christmas?" he asked, their tennis court spat evidently forgotten.

"Shush, it's a surprise," she told him, then in a whisper, "One of those fancy Spanish fans. You know, with the ivory and all."

"Oh, really." He took a thoughtful step backward. "I didn't realize she was a dancer."

"Silly, she collects them," Cindy said, shaking her head. She wasn't going to hold a grudge either.

When the tree was almost all finished, the Ambassador appeared and ascended the stepladder. Cindy handed him the little angel with the silvery wings and the job was done. Then he climbed down, kissed his two ladies, and this summed up the family feeling for the holidays as far as his daughter was concerned. She felt happiness spreading through the Embassy out into the world. Peace on earth, goodwill to all men.

Later, while dressing for the reception, Cindy's inner glow persisted, though her mother dabbed irritably at her face in the mirror of her dressing room. "This is a moment I always loathe," she said.

"Nervous, Mom?"

"Always. When I was a girl, parties made me sick. I mean physically, face-down-in-the-john sick."

"Lucky you grew out of it," Cindy said, knowing her mother hadn't really. Embassy parties, after you'd been to two or three and seen beyond the glamor, weren't designed for enjoyment. At best they were a necessary evil, allowing diplomats to pass hints, suggest deals, deliver unwritten warnings, all of it off the record, at the price of fatigue, indigestion, boredom, and sometimes scandal. Cindy had observed her mother glide through this decorous vacuum with an air of easy grace, make out the guest lists, send the invitations, circulate among the important guests, and was one of the few to know that it did not come naturally. When her mother said lightly, "You go ahead, dear. I'm supposed to be fashionably late, make the grand entrance," Cindy knew Marjory's real motive was to be alone, to collect her nerve, and, if her nerve failed, brace herself with a shot of liquor, then brush her teeth vigorously.

As Cindy well knew, it was the duty of the Embassy staff, counselors, secretaries of first, second, and third degrees, the various attachés, particularly the protocol officer, to arrive before the Ambassador and his lady. There was nothing in the protocol book about the arrival of ambassadors' daughters. Unlike her mother, Cindy, who was obliged only to smile, still enjoyed these affairs. She liked standing back imagining what was on their minds as the guests arrived bowing and grinning and the room gradually turned into a din of faces, smoke, and glassiness.

On this occasion the turnout was not large. Outside, traffic had dwindled. Many stores were closed, and not in honor of Christmas or the fact that tomorrow was the Moslem holy day as well. Of course some guests would arrive late from the West German Embassy party, very dry affairs she'd been told, in the hope that once the Saudi guests went on their way the resourceful Americans would overlook the national prohibition against alcohol and break out the contraband liquor. For now it was cola, orange juice, and a fizzy yellow fluid that tasted sweet. Cindy made a face.

"Almost like champagne," Kim said encouragingly.

"Better," Cindy insisted. "It's good for you, like cough syrup and milk of magnesia."

"I'm not saying it's better, just that it's similar," Kim replied.

By now a couple of dozen people were standing in stiff, cold groups, but the reception room remained too large for the informal mood that had been stressed. The Ambassador had appeared alone, smiling with social affability. He held his guests by the elbow, pretending to be attentive, but Cindy saw him repeatedly glancing toward the door to which he hastened when General Ibn Abdul Aziz's party was announced.

Oh, Mom, what are you doing? Cindy wondered, now that the important ones were here. It seemed to her that the new arrivals added an exotic note to the occasion, as though the Three Kings had dropped in. All save General Aziz were richly robed. He was in a severe Western-style uniform. Tall and dark, the cast of his mouth and eyes was downward, hinting at sullenness, a mood that the light and authority of his smile contradicted. His forehead bore that silvery callous, the mark of a true believer, from touching the ground during prayer. He did not seem at all the sort of man to be associated with stories of prisoners buried up to their necks in sand, waiting for the desert sun to rise. Still, such stories had made the rounds, and Cindy had heard them: "Beware Aziz, especially when he laughs."

Cindy had not anticipated being drawn into the group but evidently her father regarded her as a hostess substitute, for he beckoned her over. General Aziz took her offered hand in both of his, a very un-Arabic thing to do, and she murmured back phonetic little nothings.

"Ah, here is Colonel Mohammed Ali Rajai," said the General. "Oh, no, Miss Cooper, no need to shake hands. He is an old-fashioned Arab. He will salaam. Yes, see how graceful for an old fellow. He speaks only Arabic."

"Allah be praised," croaked Colonel Rajai in English, as if to repudiate his superior.

"Hear him," commented General Aziz. "We have great laughs with Ali Rajai. He knows all kinds of tricks. Ah, and here is the resident spy," he added, on taking note of Colonel Anderson.

"At your service, General." Colonel Anderson clicked his heels, adding, "I trust you know that your companion is an old assassin."

"Colonel Rajai? Yes, of course. Do not trust him," General Aziz said with a genial laugh.

Though it was an odd conversation, Cindy felt the ice breaking. It might be a good party yet, but good grief, Mother!

"When I was dining with the King the other day," General Aziz said, turning to Ambassador Cooper, "I brought the conversation around to . . ."

"I heard His Majesty was not well," Colonel Anderson interjected.

"No, I am happy to say all is well with the King. His worries are external ones. Once it was the British. Now we must choose between the United States and the Soviet Union. It is very difficult to decide. His Majesty feels like a fish in a tank. The British fisherman doesn't put in a hook, no, he lets the fish swim peacefully, then he turns the tap and lets the water out. Now the Russian, when he catches the hungry fish on a hook, laughs to see it squirm. But you Americans, oh, you are strange." Cindy noticed the General's stomach was jerking convulsively in what she took to be a form of self-applause. "You Americans stick your hand into the tank, pull the fish out, stamp on him, and then . . . oh, then you drop the poor creature back into the tank and begin to feed him." He paused for a polite round of laughter, then continued to make his point. "Well, you see, His Majesty is hungry, and that is why he has chosen you Americans."

"I take it you are speaking of the F-24s," said the Ambassador.

"Oh, such directness of speech, Your Excellency, but yes, so long as you bring it up, His Majesty was speaking of them, but only as a sign of good faith, you understand."

Cindy stood by in wonder, her head going back and forth like a spectator at a tennis match. Should she be privy to this? Shouldn't she make an excuse and seek out her mother, whose absence by now had surely been noted?

"Is the situation as unstable as all that?" asked Ambassador Cooper.

"What situation?" General Aziz looked around, astonished. "Your Excellency, there is no situation that I know of. A few students, a handful of rash Palestinians. Nothing to worry about. But regarding the planes, to whom should I speak on this? You, Your Excellency, or Colonel Anderson here?" General Aziz joined his fingers together, forming a cage with the union of their tips.

"We'll set up an appointment, General Aziz," said the Ambassador. "I believe you may anticipate a productive discussion. When would you like?"

"Tomorrow, I believe, is sacred to both our religions."

"Saturday, then. The afternoon?"

"Bless you, Mr. Ambassador," Aziz replied. "If only

Allah had your talents, there would be no more hungry fish in the world."

Cindy, who had been only half-listening, sighed in relief. Finally her mother had appeared, spike heels clicking down the marble foyer like ice cubes in a tall glass. Marjory had put on more makeup than she needed and had put it on badly, lots of eyeshadow that gave her a bruised look. "If you'll excuse me." She picked her way through the crowd as if she were frightened by it. Two or three groups opened like flowers to let the queen bee land but she hovered only briefly, then moved on, saying, "I'm sure General Aziz must be holding court in there somewhere. Poor General Aziz, I must cheer him up. And Colonel Rajai looks so atrociously sad."

Colonel Mohammed Ali Rajai performed his deep and graceful bow and a beaming General Aziz seized both of Marjory's hands, saying, "Madam, you honor us with your radiance once again."

"Chivalry is not dead as long as we have our splendid General Aziz," Marjory flattered back. "How well you look. But what's become of the refreshments? I don't suppose I should even suggest a sinful wee glass of vodka on the rocks? No? Then Coca-Cola it is. Plenty of ice, as I recall."

Marjory was talking too fast and too much, it seemed to Cindy, but Kim said, "Your mother's outrageous. I'd no idea. The way she gets a party going."

By now a few European diplomats had trickled in. Appetizers and soft drinks were circulating but General Aziz toyed nervously with his glass of cola and Colonel Rajai hauled from his robes a large gold watch on a silver chain and announced the time very solemnly, as if he knew a great deal more about it than anyone else. After an exchange in Arabic, the Saudis seemed about to depart.

"Please, General, you wouldn't disappoint us and leave so early?" said Marjory. She sounded genuinely heartbroken.

General Aziz smiled back rather enigmatically and replied, "I'm afraid, dear lady, the world is too much with us just now."

"But surely, General, you're not enough with us. What a shame we never hear you sing. You have such a reputation, and here it is Christmas Eve."

"Perhaps I shall sing now," General Aziz said to Marjory, and to Cindy's astonishment he did, in Arabic. His voice rose thin and high, gave out strange sounds. Occasionally Cindy suspected a rhythm, even the illusion of a Western melody, but her ears were repeatedly baffled, losing all clues, stumbling in a maze of sounds, not really unpleasant or harsh. It might have been the song of an extinct bird. General Aziz bit off the last refrain, salaamed to the ladies, then turned to Ambassador Cooper about their appointment.

"Saturday, then, if God wills," said General Aziz, taking his leave.

"What graceful people they are," the Ambassador said of the exiting Saudis.

"Graceful like cats, and just as dependable," observed Colonel Anderson.

"Dear General Aziz," said Marjory. "I do enjoy him, though I'm not sure he's quite the type we need at a Christmas party."

"You didn't have to offer him vodka," said her husband.

"Howard, I simply can't help teasing the funny man. That song of his was too much. Well, thank heavens they've gone. The rest of you must stay. It's absurdly early yet, but no more shop talk. It's Christmas Eve. Dearest, wouldn't it be all right if we brought out something wet? I would so adore an utterly dry vodka martini."

Ever since the shooting of a British consul by a Saudi citizen demanding liquor from the British Embassy's private stock, alcohol had been forbidden even to the diplomatic corps in Saudi Arabia. Cindy knew this as well as she knew that it was still smuggled in on the military transport planes from Frankfurt, or offered on the black market at upward of a hundred dollars a bottle. The American Embassy was no exception, the only real problem being disposal of the empties, which had to be broken down into unrecognizable chips before being put out with the garbage.

Once the group was reduced to the Embassy staff only, the liquor began to flow, vodka martinis and white wine. Cindy mistook a glass of the former for wine and to conceal her inexperience drained the glass in one gulp. She didn't sputter or choke but her eyes teared and for a moment she could scarcely speak. Marjory, with her solitary head start, held a martini in both hands before her like a consecrated grail. Under Cindy's critical gaze she seemed to be undergoing a conspicuous metamorphosis. One eyelid had begun to droop ever so slightly. The lines in her face deepened and her laughter, intended as coyly flirtatious, sounded like chalk on a blackboard.

Catching her daughter's scrutiny, Marjory said, "Am I talking too much, dear? I'm not, am I?" Not waiting for an answer, she added, "That General Aziz. I wonder if he's as silly as he seems, or does he simply pretend to be."

"What do you think, Anderson?" asked the Ambassador.

"Hard to say," replied the Colonel, as if he knew the answer and wasn't about to spill a military secret. And then, in imitation of Aziz's Oxford accent, "I am happy to inform you that our army and its equipment are all A-number one, and I can tell you in strictest confidence that we have a nuclear device. Yes, it is true, blessings to be Allah. It was made locally in the bazaar. We found a very clever chap, a tinsmith."

Laughter spread contagiously until the Ambassador remarked, "I wouldn't underrate those tinsmiths. And Anderson, I think we had better be prepared to juggle our friend Aziz for a bit. Handing over the F-24s just now doesn't make a great deal of sense to me."

"It makes sense to the President and his advisers."

"Then I believe we must try to show them better sense, Colonel."

Again Cindy listened back and forth. It seemed unlikely fare for a Christmas party. And who, when she thought about it, could talk seriously about someone who warbled like a bird. Of much greater concern was her mother and what she seemed to be doing to herself in public.

"Why can't we have some dance music?" Marjory exclaimed from her couch. An aide obliged, and the murmur of the Westminster Choir gave way to the strident beat out of China that had supplanted disco and rock. Some called it chop-suey jazz, or just "suey." Marjory rose in response, caught her heel, and nearly fell. She sat down again, saying, "Oh, my, perhaps I need a drink first." While the staff pretended blindness, neither Cindy nor her father could. "Will you look at my poor husband's face? I've done it again, haven't I? I've had one too many, but in a place like this"—she turned toward Cindy in appeal—"what else can you do?"

"Mom, please," Cindy pleaded, and from her father, "Marjory, this doesn't become you. If you imagine you have escaped observation—"

Marjory's blue eyes brimmed, tremulous, overflowed as she stared at him. Mascara began to wash down. "You pompous SOB," she said with drunken care.

A scene was about to erupt and Cindy knew it. "Mom,

let's go on up." Cindy offered her arm and surprisingly her mother took it. "Show me the way to go home," Marjory sang in a sort of self-imitation while the staff talked about the weather. "Yes, show me the way to go home," she sang louder, beginning to cry again, but by now they were out of the reception hall and on the way upstairs. There Marjory insisted she had never been better. "Go back to the party, dear. For heaven's sake, have a good time for both of us," she insisted.

Cindy very much wanted to have a good time. Champagne was being passed out when she got back, and Kim offered her a glass. "Care to dance?" A slow foxtrot was playing.

"I like this old-fashioned stuff," she said, putting a hand on his shoulder. "Say, you're good."

"So are you."

They danced silently.

"Your mom okay?"

"She just wishes she was back in New England this time of year."

"That'd be nice for tonight. Snowing but very still," Kim said. "My mom's there now. I mean, that's where the place is. I usually at least get a Christmas letter."

"Did you send her one?"

Kim nodded, then in a near-breathless whisper, "Weeks ago." Brightening with a visible effort he added, "Look at the old man over there, cutting loose." His voice was genial but his face was stony.

"He's some dancer," Cindy agreed.

"Well, let's do it," Kim said, and whirled her away to the music. Cindy began to feel happy and relaxed. When the music was interrupted Kim fumbled in his breast pocket with fingers that were long and slender and seldom out of sight, saying, "I almost forgot. Merry Christmas." His smile was slightly impertinent and rather flirtatious.

Embarrassed, Cindy opened the small gift box. Bedded in cotton was a spun-glass camel. "I don't deserve this," she said, having nothing to give in return. "When did you get it?"

"This morning, and I think you do, just because you're the most deliciously pretty girl I've seen in weeks."

"Am I?" The gift was embarrassing but not the compliment. Cindy simply widened her smile. Then she bobbed forward, bestowing a light kiss on Kim's cheek.

"Hey, that's the way chipmunks kiss." He put his arms around her and did his best to exact tribute for the camel, but she twisted her head away with a little gasp.

"I don't think that's necessary, Kim, though it was sweet of you to think of the camel." Not wanting to end on a huffy note, she added, "I think your father's great. What a sense of humor." But when she thought about it, she knew she didn't really care for Colonel Anderson. He was handsome enough, but he was creepy, too. There was a rumor that he'd had a glass eye since Vietnam, but if true, she couldn't figure out which one it was. They were both so cold.

"You're a weird kid," Kim said at last.

"Old-fashioned in some ways."

"You'd be a bloody bore if you weren't so damned cute," he told her, suave as hell, and Cindy knew then for sure that Kim was not her type either. He was handsome, almost too handsome. And the way he'd come on like a red-hot lover as though he meant to prove something, not to her but to himself. Deep down she had the suspicion that what he really needed was mothering. Well, emotional maturity wasn't her strong suit, and yet as they stood facing each other waiting for the music she had a feeling that had come once or twice before of peculiar closeness, not attraction but a kind of bonding, as though they were shipwrecked on a desert island together, not necessarily wanting to be together but together because that was how fate had worked things out.

"I ought to check on Mom," she said. "Back in a sec."

Cindy hoped to find her mother asleep, but Marjory was sitting up in bed. "A penny for your thoughts, Mom."

Marjory half-smiled. "I was remembering our wedding. Howard went down the aisle in creaking shoes," she said, glowering into her half-empty glass. "You know, I don't need this stuff, I just like it."

"You ought to get some sleep, Mom. I could plump up the pillows."

Ignoring the offer, Marjory replied, "Sweetheart, will you pass me those cigaboos?" Reluctantly Cindy complied. Her mother lit a match, couldn't get it and the cigarette to connect. Cindy steadied her hand. Marjory took a deep draft. "God, how I loathe this place. I loathe the beastly climate. I loathe the bloody wogs, must never call them that. Why wasn't your father posted to London? Now I'm being so much help to poor old Howard we're bound to end up in Chad or the North Pole. Do the beastly Eskimos have an embassy, I wonder?" Marjory toyed thoughtfully with her glass, then poured its contents down her throat angrily. Her eyes glittered with tears.

"Mom, are you okay?"

"I let your father down tonight. The hostess with the mostest thought she was doing just fine, and then she saw this loud, tiresome, middle-aged shrew across the room. She asked herself, 'Who is that shrill creature?' and you know what, she was staring into one of those wall mirrors. But it wasn't me, not really, was it? How could it be?"

Now the tears flowed unrestrainedly and Marjory surrendered the empty glass without resistance, then the cigarette, which Cindy stubbed out. She began stroking her mother's hair and trying to reassure her. "It wasn't that bad, Mom. Honestly, Kim thought you were just great with the Saudis. What if I give you a back rub—would that help?"

Marjory submitted to this and presently she stopped crying and wondered aloud, "Do you remember those Christmases in Massachusetts when you were little?"

"Of course I do, Mom."

"Or is it just that I've told you so often? We had such fun."

Marjory fell silent again and this time Cindy knew by her steady breathing that she was asleep. Cindy sat on the edge of the bed for a moment, took a deep, rather tremulous breath. "Good night, Mom," she whispered, and turned off the light.

No longer in a party mood, Cindy still returned to the reception room for the sake of appearances. By now the gathering had thinned to a determined hard core. The first secretary's wife was offering to recite.

"She used to be in the theater," Kim said.

"Oh."

"Summer stock. She wants to do the prayer of Montezuma to the sun."

"What does that have to do with Christmas?"

Kim shrugged. "They say she does it very dramatically."

"Oh, Montezuma! Montezuma!" the first secretary's wife began in a ringing soprano. My head's spinning, Cindy thought. If I don't cry soon I'll begin to laugh like a hyena.

The recitation was followed by a perfunctory round of puzzled applause and Colonel Anderson's loud announcement that it was the season to be jolly and time to sing carols. "Hark the Herald Angels!" he demanded in a tone of savagery as though he meant to punish Christmas and its retinue of wise men, shepherds, and holy families.

That was how Christmas Eve ended, with the singing of carols and Kim urging Cindy to sing louder. “I can’t hear you,” he intoned, “fa-la-la-la-la,” but it wasn’t until the last song with Colonel Anderson shouting the lead that they really got going. “God Bless America” volleyed round the echoing room and out into the dark Arabian night where all the icy stars glared down.

7

"Still holding up, Cindy?" said Doctor Harper. "This has been one hell of a long session."

In fact Cindy was exhausted. Her head pounded but she didn't want to admit it. She was ready for a fight.

"I'd feel better if the air weren't so strange," she said. "It tastes second hand."

"I'm afraid I can't help that," Doctor Harper apologized.

"I might think better," she argued. "Why can't you find me a room with a window?" Then it came again, that image of splintering glass. She grimaced, her eyes shut so tightly she saw sparks.

"Cindy, what's wrong?" exclaimed the doctor, his hand to her forehead.

"Nothing," she replied, startled by his concern. "It's all right; it's passed." Her memories were sparse and distorted like shreds of mist in a dark night. "Don't ships still have portholes?"

"Luxury ships, but we don't have what you'd regard as first-class accommodations, Cindy."

"And it's so still, always?" she pressed on doggedly. "We never seem to travel anywhere. Is the crew ashore? This is a warship, isn't it, Doctor Harper?"

"As a matter of fact, yes, you're right," Harper admitted,

and the readiness of his answer more than the admission itself surprised her.

"And you're a U.S. Navy doctor?"

Harper nodded assent, adding, "Specializing in psychiatric medicine, and I think it would be a good idea to move along to the day of the attack. Step by step, if you can remember."

"Why always me?" Cindy wondered. "Somebody must be questioning the others. They're so much more in the know."

"Cindy, I realize how tired you are, how hard this is. Believe me, it's not only for the information. From the medical point of view, which concerns me personally, we want to make you a whole person again, and you won't be until you come to grips with what happened," Harper explained.

"And there isn't anyone else from the Embassy here?"

"Not to my knowledge, Cindy. At least you're the only survivor assigned to me."

"What do you mean, survivor?"

"Witness, if you like."

"The only witness," Cindy echoed.

"Aboard this craft."

Suddenly she felt so alone and vulnerable, needing so badly about her, like a wall, the people who loved her—Mom and Dad, her grandparents, and their big old golden retriever because nothing loved like a dog—that she began to cry silently, simply oozing tears. But there wasn't anyone who cared, except Doctor Harper, maybe a little, so it surprised her again when he stroked her hair as she had consoled her mother Christmas Eve, and even more to see tears glistening in his eyes, too.

Finally Cindy said, "I think I'm okay now, if you want to go on with the attack on the Embassy."

"Only if you're absolutely up to it."

"You'll want the recorder on," she said, depressing the play button. "Shall I start with Christmas Day?"

While the tree glowed, life should be protected somehow. Only good could enter the Embassy. At Christmas nothing could change and nobody could worry. Everyone had to be loving at Christmas. Cindy had believed as a little girl that people's souls were put on a scale at Christmastime, and those who were good received sleds and ice skates and pretty new clothes while, according to her grandmother, the wicked found nothing but a lump of coal in their stocking. That night, alone in bed, Cindy had imagined a new-fallen snow on the ground and she had prayed that she might confront all the evil in the world alone. If she won, none would be left, and if she failed she alone would suffer. What presumption, she thought even then, but of course it was Christmas Eve.

The next morning the real world had returned with rumors, the most disturbing of which was that the King was at the point of death. Reports kept being delivered to her father from the Foreign Broadcast Information Service. The Saudi army and air force were mobilizing. True? False? At the Embassy they had to wait, while playing out the comedy of seeming to wait for nothing at all. The Cooper family exchanged presents. Marjory seemed genuinely delighted with the Spanish fan. The Ambassador was distracted, kept being called from the room. Cindy suspected he'd had little sleep.

"Are things really bad?" Cindy asked him.

"I wish I knew, sweetheart," he replied. "I'll have a better idea after I've talked to Aziz tomorrow."

But when Saturday came, General Aziz failed, without

explanation, to keep his appointment. The struggle in the city remained indefinable, yet strong enough to paralyze. Businesses failed to reopen after the Friday holy day closing, and there was almost no traffic. It was too quiet until, as inconspicuously at first as a change in barometric pressure, something happened. For Cindy it began when a strange fear crept over her flesh. She felt it as a stirring among the roots of her hair. She and her parents had just started lunch when, not knowing why, she sat erect, listening, and then she realized it was the distant sound of a crowd, thousands of voices shouting. "They'll be banging their heads together out there," her father said coolly. "It often happens." When Cindy had gained a window view, the avenue beyond the compound gates appeared paved with heads. A placard reading "Hands off Saudi Arabia" was jerked up and down, and a cardboard effigy of Uncle Sam began to burn. Finally a small car was overturned. Rocks began pelting over the wall until, with a noise like an earthquake, a platoon of Saudi tanks trundled nose to tail down the avenue, sweeping away the mob.

All essential Embassy personnel, counselors, code clerks, anyone on private holiday, began trickling in through the back door. Reluctantly the Embassy was going on restricted alert, for it seemed premature to spread a wider alarm. That afternoon Ambassador Cooper called a conference with his senior staff. Cindy heard his statement second-hand. The last thing he wanted was to precipitate a panic by overreaction. They had been invited by the Saudi government to give military and civil training and advice. They had sold the Saudi government most of the military equipment it had requested. That was all. They had not requested or been given any authority to intervene in the internal politics of a sovereign state. Their hands, in short, were tied, and the Embassy was not to be confused with the pass at Thermopylae. There would be no fight to the death.

"But it is American soil, sir," Colonel Anderson had interjected.

"Theoretically, Anderson, only theoretically. So was our Embassy in Tehran. If there's going to be a war, if we are to become involved, it isn't to start here."

Such was the Ambassador's official policy. He had something else to say to Cindy in private. She knew from his expression, which suggested a diplomatic note if not an ultimatum, that she wouldn't enjoy what she heard. "I requested, as a matter of extreme urgency, to talk with the King," he told her, "and very politely I was informed that he was in conference and not to be disturbed."

"I thought he was deathly ill," Cindy said.

"It's when stories don't jibe that I begin to worry. Anyway, what I'm getting around to is, we have one of our Air Force planes standing by with pouches at the airport. It's a routine flight tomorrow morning. You and your mother and the other dependents will be aboard. You'll be flown out there by helicopter."

"Helicopter!"

"Right from the tennis courts. Should be a lark."

"So it's really dangerous," Cindy said, remembering the crisis at the Embassy in Tehran and the letters she and her grade-school classmates had written to the hostages there.

"Now you're being a bit romantic." Howard Cooper tapped his teeth with a pen. "You must understand these desert Arabs. It's words more than facts that get them going, and they have a word, 'fantasia.' Fantasia seems to be brewing here. Picture a Bedouin sitting motionless for hours, contemplating the desert. Suddenly he explodes into action. He gallops his camel through the village, fires off his gun. Others begin racing around, shooting. It's a contagious wildness and when they get really wound up, the target can be anything that moves. It shouldn't be our fight at all. We're only observers. Must stay out of harm's way, that's all."

Cindy knew his air of nonchalance was false. "Then why the chopper, Dad?"

"Airports, and the roads to them, have a disconcerting way of shutting down, old dear. It's easier to get there with a chopper, that's all."

"So when do we have to be ready exactly?"

"Nineish. You'll have plenty of time to pack. No rush."

"I feel an awful deserter, Dad." When she was small, the American Ambassador to Afghanistan had been killed. "I don't want you left behind here. Please, Dad."

"You know the answer to that. I only wish I'd had a bit more foresight before Christmas. I don't know . . . the whole thing's more than I bargained for. Well." He put his hands on his knees, preparatory to standing up. "Things to do." He turned to the door. "And sweetheart, I suppose it's best if we keep the evacuation business mum for now."

So the vacation was over. Less than twenty-four hours and she'd be gone. Cindy scarcely knew whether to be sorry or to breathe a sigh of relief. If Dad weren't staying behind, like the captain of a sinking ship, it would be all right. It had been fun in a way, like running along the edge of a high cliff, exhilarating while it lasted. Now to be flown out by helicopter—really, there'd be stories to tell at school. But all that was spoiled as long as her father remained in danger. Better that they all be together and take their chances together. Reluctantly she began to pack, pausing at the sound of dry sticks burning. Gunfire? Seeking confirmation, she went outside into the compound where Colonel Anderson pounded around the tennis court with one of the stenographers. His long, pale ostrich legs propelled him with great bounds. Hadn't he heard the shots, or was this some sort of all-is-normal routine to keep the staff calm? She wondered if Kim was packing to go and would have looked him up had she not run into Salim.

"Oh, sorry, I didn't see you," she said as he emerged from the palms.

"Miss Cindy, how nice. Was the Christmas party good, I hope?"

"So-so," she replied, very glad that he had not been there for the jokes and to see Marjory in action. "You mustn't let me forget to give you those stamps for your collection."

"Yes, thank you, they would be very nice. If I may make very bold, Miss Cindy—I'm sorry, Cindy—before you go back to school, for us to try a game of tennis."

"I wish there were time," she apologized.

"No time? I am very good at memory, Cindy. You have ten days, am I not correct?"

"Well, yes and no." She cast about for a lie. "Mom and I were talking about a few days in Europe, shopping, doing the museums." The rule was, if you're going to tell a lie, make it good or quick with authority. She hadn't quite succeeded in this and Salim gave her an odd look. "Of course, it's not absolutely set. If there's time, I'd love a game." She glanced at the red sky. "It's too late today, don't you think?"

"Yes," Salim agreed, "today is over." He seemed suddenly in a hurry as if awakening to the memory of an appointment. "May you sleep well and waken in goodness."

"Yes, you too," she replied as he hurried off. Get back inside, she told herself, before you blab everything. He guessed, I'm sure he guessed. It was as though Salim had entrapped her, knowing to the day the length of her vacation, or perhaps it was only a guess based on last year.

Her father was holding a staff meeting so Cindy ate alone with her mother. Marjory was unashamedly elated, an unexpected visit to Europe, just the two of them. She was engrossed in Fodor's *Italy 1987* when Cindy excused herself. She didn't want to be with her mother just then, and she had to wonder about her parents' marriage that, at least until Christmas Eve, had always shown to her such a clearness of shape and purpose. Inside her own room, Cindy considered locking the door for the first time but found no key. Surely there had been one. After laying out travel clothes, she undressed and pulled on a nightgown. At that moment from one of the minarets a muezzin began calling the faithful to prayer, his wailing voice sounding as eerie as a coyote in the desert. Cindy drifted to the window. So many stars; she would never get used to them. No wonder the Bedouin had become the great astronomers of ancient times. Cindy yawned and stretched, her small breasts thrust hard against the sheer nylon, while on the night air the muezzin's voice lingered, more felt than heard. Gazing into the lower darkness of the palm court she saw the first jet flickering of the bats. Deep blue and green shadows moved there, and amid the shadows a figure stood, as if on guard. She knew somehow that the hazy figure was Salim. Cindy waved, and as at the passing of a magician's wand the figure disappeared, not gone so much as vanished. Was he embarrassed at being caught there staring up at her window? It wasn't as though she were naked. Only her shoulders were bare. Really, Cindy decided, how silly. She must have looked quite nice.

A smouldering Arabian moon began rising over the compound. At first Cindy mistook it for a fire burning in the city until it cleared the rooftops. The rays of the December moon were cold, and she shivered, yearning for the feather bed she'd left at Le Rosey. She was about to turn away when something smacked into the roof above the window. The tiles might have been contracting with the cold but deep down she felt it had been a bullet. Fired at random in some distant street scuffle, or aimed at the Embassy in general, or at her, silhouetted there?

Within seconds she had the light extinguished. Oddly calm, Cindy lay in bed. Sleep refused to come. Her throat was dry and dusty and she smelled something like pepper in her nose, as though she'd received a blow and the little blood vessels were broken. Anything was better than to be dead on the floor, an undiscovered international incident, with that destiny she had always supposed for herself to unfold postmortem. "I'm not ready to be dead," she said aloud. She'd always talked to herself, a childish habit, but what harm did it do? No, damn it, she had too much to discover yet, mainly about herself. She knew the outward Cindy pretty well: good student, particularly in literature and art. No Picasso, no inventor of a new style, but good enough, maybe, to paint pleasant wall decorators. Competent tennis player, maybe a mixed doubles championship at the club, but no Wimbledon battler. Popular enough, no trouble with dates. Healthy, first-rate insurance risk, typical teenager experimenting with blond streaks in her hair and pierced ears, comfortable in navy blue cardigans and cable-knit knee socks. "What a bore. Really, I'm just a preppy bore like Kim. It wouldn't matter a bit if we were both dead. Except to me, and to Mom and Dad."

Behind that facade was another Cindy, an unfinished version that cried sometimes, not knowing why. Because people got older and things changed? There was a Cindy who feared involvement, wanted to be left alone, wanting at the same time fiercely to be needed, to do something worthwhile, a wish so presumptuous she could barely admit it to herself. She wanted somehow to fulfill the old cliché and make the world a better place. Marriage and children? Babies didn't excite her the way they did some of her friends. Was this selfishness? Was she as interested in boys as she sometimes pretended to be? Not really. Maybe she was emotionally retarded. She'd had plenty of crushes. She'd had a fleeting passion for Kim. He was so good looking and so awfully rude. Probably just what she deserved, but you had to really like people before you could love them. She loved her parents, her father particularly just now, maybe because he seemed so calmly courageous in the face of danger. "Oh, God," she whispered, though no churchgoer or true believer, "if you're there and if you care, look after my father. Don't let anything bad happen. And if there's any sense in what's going on, let me understand." Surely it made no sense to meet a stray bullet in an alien city in the middle of Saudi Arabia.

"I can hardly imagine being shot at and going straight to bed," Doctor Harper asked. "Weren't you frightened?"

"I was shocked. It didn't seem real," Cindy said. "I'm more afraid now than I was then."

"You have nothing to fear from us," he told her, the words so bland, and yet behind them lurked something that seemed harried and desperate.

"It's not you," she said, "it's what's hidden inside me. Well, and it's the atmosphere, too. It's so incredibly still and quiet. If I only had a clue to where we were. Doctor?"

"Cindy, you're going to think I'm being deliberately

mysterious, but I'm not. I'd be exceeding my authority if I said. I think we're in the Indian Ocean, and I might be wrong by now. It's classified. I'm a doctor, and I'm simply not privy to that sort of information." He leaned forward and squeezed her hand. "The most important thing just now, as far as I'm concerned, is your well-being. Please believe that."

Cindy did not question his concern. The doctor was like her father in generating confidence, but the situation itself did not add up. Pieces were missing or did not fit together, and she could not entirely attribute this feeling to her still-blurred memory.

"Where do you come from originally, Doctor Harper?"

Painstakingly labeling a cassette with a ballpoint pen, Harper turned in surprise. "Pardon? I'm sorry, these things never write."

"Your home."

"San Diego, I suppose, when I'm not floating around."

"You sound sort of, I don't know, English," she said. "Maybe a little Slavic, too, if you don't mind my saying so."

"Wow!" Doctor Harper rocked back in his chair. "You're beginning to frighten me now. As a matter of fact, my parents came from Hungary. I studied and did a residency in London. You're one hell of a perceptive young lady." He gave the recorder a shake. "Damn!"

"Harper isn't exactly a Hungarian name," Cindy pressed on. "By the way, I'd try plugging it in—the tape recorder, that is."

"Sound idea," he agreed. "Why don't we trade places? Good, I knew you probably knew how to smile. But anyway, Cindy, to answer your question, my family name was very long and unpronounceable, so my parents had it changed. Now, much as I'd prefer to gab with you, I'm afraid we ought to get back to business. You'd just been shot at."

Usually Cindy went to sleep quickly, the way you turn off a light: she'd simply squirm around until she'd snuggled into a comfortable cocoon and then with a faint smile her breath would begin to purr softly. That night she'd thought about her life nearly being over before it had begun until she drifted off slowly into a convoluted maze of shallow and unrefreshing dreams. Quick footsteps in the corridor made her stir, and behind her closed lids strange shapes lurked and watched. A fitful murmur rising from the city blended drowsily with her reveries and she dreamed of a mob, a mob she could never quite see, like a shadow or fatal mist gathering outside the window, behind the trees in the courtyard. She could hear them breathing, advancing again, flowing like lava. Cindy woke with a start and the smell of something acrid burning in her nostrils. She squinted into the darkness. Why was it so dark? Someone was there.

"Mom?"

"It's Salim bin-Kabina, Miss Cindy."

Cindy froze. The most startling aspect of the Arab's sudden reappearance, more difficult for Cindy to accept than an act of magic, was the simple flesh-and-blood fact of his being there. It was unthinkable.

"What's going on!" she demanded. "What are you doing in my room?"

"You must get up and come with me, please," he said.

There was enough predawn light now for her to see that he held a gun of some sort, enough for him to see the shock and outrage and growing terror in her face. Despite the deadly weapon in Salim's hands, Cindy sensed that he was nearly as alarmed as she, because girls were supposed to be plump, liquid eyed, opaquely veiled, and compliant, and here was the Ambassador's daughter, a pale, fierce reality in a flimsy gown that did not leave much to the imagination.

Relying on this hesitancy, Cindy took hold of her fear and resolved to brazen through. "Salim, do you realize you could lose your job?" Her eyes looked very large, not so much frightened as proud. "Go away and I won't say anything. Salim!" They stood staring. "All right, then get out of my way. I'm leaving," and she marched right at him. Salim held his ground. Cindy kept on until they were face to face. "Out of the way!" His cheeks burned at the thought of having to grab her arm. "I'm going to see my parents."

"You won't find them," he said, gaining the advantage, stiffening, then relenting. "They are already in custody. They are safe."

"Then get out! This is my room." Her voice sounded cracked now, desperate.

"Better me than one of the others. Miss Cindy, you will please dress." Salim spoke quietly, but it sounded harsher than he intended. "There, put these on." And he held up the clothes she had laid out for the flight. Cindy seized hold of them, started for the bathroom, but they shared the same thought. "No!" he commanded. "You will lock yourself in."

"If you're expecting some sort of private peep show . . ."

"I am looking out the window," he said. "Now dress, please."

In the end they compromised. The clothes closet had no lock, and she changed in there. Good stiff jeans and a pullover sweater made her feel more secure, and dressing gave her time to think. "What's the meaning of this?" she demanded through the door, grasping for the outrage and strength to mask the tremor in her voice. "What's going on? Who are the others?"

"We are many," he explained. Now Salim held all the cards. He played them with relief. "We are an army, though we do not all wear uniforms. We wish for this homeland of ours to be a republic. We would die that it be so." He delivered these lines with reverence, as a priest might render a liturgical chant, almost sung, going a bit beyond his breath so he had to gasp for the next.

He's some kind of fanatic, Cindy realized as she pulled on her sneakers. Given a chance to run, she'd run.

"Are you the leader?" she asked.

"General Aziz commands us."

The funny man who sang like a bird? Cindy was incredulous.

"And may I say on his behalf that we are very sorry to so inconvenience our American friends."

"Do what?" She was dressed now and had regained a good deal of spunk.

"Hold the Embassy hostage, but you see, your army and your secret agents must not intervene. Fear nothing. You are safe."

"Then why the gun?"

"If we could be sure of success, Miss Cindy, by strewing rose petals, that would be nicer. The guns are temporary. No one will be hurt."

"No one's ever hurt," she replied contemptuously, "only dead."

"Please, you Americans are our guests. There is a proverb, that when one receives a guest one receives Allah as well. As soon as your President recognizes our new government, all will be well. The King is overthrown. Even now, all is under control. Have no fear. We Arabs have a word, 'karama.' You would say, honor. Better to die with honor than live in humiliation. For me, it means I would die to keep you safe." Ready to die, ready to kill. Cindy had met her first revolutionary. She shivered, wanting to be with her parents. "Now come, you will be better in the center of the compound." She didn't understand, so he tried to explain. "Is a man wise to cut down the tree that gives him fruit? For us, your country is that tree, yet some factions want nothing to do with America. They would spit on you for the sake of their self-esteem. That would be dangerous, and so we must go to the safest place, and you must go with your hands tied."

"Tied? What can I do?"

"It is the rule," Salim apologized. "Not mine. I will not tie them tightly. Please."

Cindy gave in and presented her wrists together as though already manacled.

"This is very sad for me," he said while doing the job. "That does not hurt, surely. Good, now come along, please. You have no choice. Come this way."

The palm court was filled with shadowy figures, ghostly in long white robes and headcloths. They looked extraordinarily tense and ready to leap at any offense, and they were all armed.

Salim led her across the tennis court. There, a crowd of young Arabs were taking turns hacking away at the flagpole with an ax. Finally the ax was handed to an old man with a long gray beard. His strokes were feeble but all that was needed. The flag sank, as if dying. The old man shouted something out loud in Cindy's direction.

"What did he say?" she demanded of Salim.

"That the people are now master of their destiny."

There was cobra venom in the ancient's eyes as Salim led his captive by, and he spat on the ground, saying, "Al

Na Srain!" a chant the others took up. Cindy did not ask this time. She knew it meant "Christian."

"Yallah, yallah—hurry," Salim urged her. "These are fanatics," and as he said it she saw the glint of a sword being drawn in the first onrush of sunlight.

Remembering that sword, and later another, blood red at another dawning, she cried out. Doctor Harper leaned close with his microphone, demanding, "Cindy, what is it? What is it about the tennis courts that you remember? Tell me!" Her head rolled back and forth on the pillow, her hands fluttering in protest. "Try," Harper urged. "Perhaps you can't remember now because you don't want to. Try, Cindy."

"It's nothing. It's only a dream," she insisted.

"Tell me what you see in the dream."

"I see the sword glinting. I see a grave. No . . . No!" Now she knew it had to be a dream, for she seemed to see the Embassy compound below, rapidly diminishing, but not the compound as she knew it, in its place a smouldering ruin. Her face was pinched in an agony of concentration. In the dream she was being carried. She heard a voice say, "Carefully, she's badly hurt," and then the whomp-whomp of great rotors and a bumping, lurching ride into unconsciousness. Her mind reeled back into the present. Harper was holding a glass to her lips. "Thank you. I'm sorry," she told him, her eyes filling with belated tears that tracked down her face.

"After what you've been through," the doctor replied, "tears are the best medicine. Let them come, Cindy."

8

"Doctor Harper, is it you or someone else who is keeping me here?" Cindy asked.

"Medically speaking, Cindy, I couldn't in good conscience recommend your release, not while your memory's impaired."

"But that's not the whole story, is it?"

"No. I'm not in charge of security decisions. Please get some sleep now," he urged her. "You've had a bad time. You must pace yourself. I'll be back in an hour or two. Trust me, Cindy."

The door closed with the heavy click of a safe-deposit vault. She was sealed in a small, anonymous box on an unnamed ship, God knew where. Under closed lids Cindy rolled her eyes high. She did not want to sleep, for in sleep she floundered in a kind of dream prison where frightening surprises lurked. Keep thinking. What if it weren't a U.S. Navy ship? There were so few clues. The doctor's accent—he said he was originally Hungarian. Russian? Cindy fought against sleep, trying to think, but the drug was strong and she was weak. The bandage on her wrist was still unexplained. Could things yet unremembered have been so bad that she tried to take her life? "I'm not the suicidal type," she said half-aloud, her words slurring. She'd never become reconciled to death, couldn't understand what it meant. At times she nearly could, but then it would fade, a picture seen through rippling water. She would visualize her own corpse, that was easy, but always she was the one to see it, with her living eyes, and this frightening vision had come again and again during those first hours of being a prisoner at the Embassy in Riyadh.

Salim had hurried her behind the tennis courts into one of the buildings intended to house single women on the Embassy staff who elected to live within the compound. It was now packed to overflowing. Salim had left her there, stunned, too confused and frightened to make a fuss. After a while, she'd wandered about, asking for her parents, but no one knew where the Ambassador and his wife might be. There were, in fact, no men at all except for a few armed Saudi guards. By mid-afternoon of that first day, all the younger women connected with the Embassy, married or not, had been brought here. Their Arab guards unloaded stacks of thin, gray, stained mattresses on the floor of the building's common room. The bedding appeared to come from a hospital ward, and it added a dreary note of permanence to the situation. On the second floor, single rooms were forced to hold three. Cindy was shunted into one of the larger double bedrooms. She was too numb to care, too confused and frightened to eat when sandwiches and tea were brought round toward dusk.

In the beginning, Cindy was constantly afraid. Emotions, thoughts, all narrowed to a sharp edge of terror. Hours, then days passed, and she was still alive. This had happened before in Iran, somewhere in Central America. After a while she could tell herself very calmly, Tomorrow at this time there is a chance you'll be dead, but probably you'll just be bored. Tedium grew with the passing days, excruciating as a dull toothache, the creeping hours with hands tied, segregated in what became known as the women's freshmen dorm. Her companions were secretaries, computer operators, a physician, two cultural liaison officers—all older than Cindy yet still disturbingly deferential to the Ambassador's daughter. For the most part, Cindy kept to herself. It would soon be over, that was the growing rumor. Salim had been right—the revolution was a success, bound up tight and tied with a bow. Loudspeaker trucks bellowed up and down the avenue in front of the Embassy, "Long live the Unity of the Popular Forces. Long live General Aziz. Glory to the heroes of the nation fallen in the struggle to win our freedom."

Soon after the Embassy seizure, victorious General Aziz paid them a visit. He was no longer the wheedling, genial clown of Christmas Eve. "We have a moral obligation to let the world know our protest matters," he'd begun, all business, pausing emphatically to hold their attention while that sank in, glancing from one American to another to assess their reaction. Cindy could feel the force of his personality shooting out into the crowd like sparks from an anvil. What had become of the bird man? "This is a crucial moment in the history of a nation searching for its final liberation. Our people wish to be the author of their own destiny." That sounded odd to Cindy, since the loudspeakers had been announcing final victory as an established fact. "In order to exercise this inalienable right," General Aziz continued, "we must not be deterred by the manipulation, the traps, or even the direct intervention of American imperialism. Once our domestic goals are achieved, rest assured we wish only the most cordial relationship with the great American people."

The bright side of General Aziz's visit was that Cindy

saw her parents in the crowd. She clumsily waved her bound hands, but was not allowed to cross the tennis courts. Afterward, as a consolation, her baggage was brought in a truck full of luggage, though it wasn't much use with her hands tied. Worse was the implication of the speech itself. Even Salim had stopped talking of the end achieved. Now it was the end at hand.

The days dragged on. Cindy asked one of the guards why they were still denied access to a bathroom, why the covered pail in the corridor didn't have disinfectant, why it wasn't emptied more often. The man seemed to speak very little English, and eventually Salim appeared. Cindy repeated her complaints to him. "We're going mad, cooped up here. Can't we walk around on the tennis court, inside the fence?" She moved close to Salim, holding out her bound wrists. "Salim, I don't weigh a hundred pounds stark naked. How can I be dangerous?"

"I will take them off for a few minutes," Salim offered.

Untied, Cindy rubbed her hands to let him know how uncomfortable she had been. "Salim, what about the other women?"

"Only you," he said.

So she made him tie them up again.

"Would you like to walk in the corridor?" Salim offered, and she walked to and fro there, feeling caged, back and forth, back and forth. She didn't want to talk with Salim, so she began to hum.

"I like that song," he said.

"Do you really?"

"I do, yes, very much, Cindy."

"Then I don't anymore," she informed him.

"I wouldn't have it this way," Salim pleaded. "I didn't think . . ."

"That it would go on so long?"

Clearly the victory of General Aziz's revolution had not been immediate. For a while Cindy's heart pounded alarm at each vague new report as her brain tried to decide what weight it cast in the scale measuring their chances for survival. Telephone communications were cut throughout the country. The rebels were sweeping south in the morning, being thrown back to the old town and part of Embassy Row in the afternoon. She strained to hear the sound of guns. Did it mean, that distant firing, a last stand or a victory celebration? Silence might mean victory, defeat, or simple stalemate between the opposing forces.

One of the secretaries, Edith somebody, made it her business to deliver reports. One day the King was back in the outskirts of Riyadh, his National Guard posed for the death blow to the rebels. The United States, Edith said, had sent His Majesty massive supplies, and the hostages in the Embassy were to be shot. Later in the day came word that the American government was only considering such aid, and the hostages were safe. The United Nations was considering the Saudi situation in general debate. Where did Edith hear all this, confined as she was? Yet Cindy listened with a despairing yet eager ear, knowing that the rumors were contradictory if not groundless. What else was there besides such figments to weigh over and over again, figments that, as time went by, indicated only one clear fact: the revolution was far from over; indeed, it hung in the balance.

While the fighting went on, gradual reforms took place in the Embassy. First, the tying of the hostages' hands was abandoned. Salim took credit for this, saying, "So you see, Cindy, we are not savages after all." She smiled obligingly, thinking to herself, Oh yes, you are. Yes, you are. Prompted by the Ambassador, a list of complaints was made up and allegedly passed on to General Aziz: inadequate bath and toilet facilities; food that was too spicy, starchy, and greasy for American consumption; lack of exercise and recreation; inability of the staff to communicate within the compound and with the outside world, though they knew this last would not be granted. A hunger strike in the senior women's dorm led to the first concession, the rehiring of the old kitchen staff. Other concessions followed. To Cindy's delight, the bathrooms were reopened, and a daily schedule was posted, far more liberal than she might have hoped. Up at 6 A.M., breakfast for the men in the cafeteria at 6:45, for the women at 7:15, followed by an hour of recreation for each sex in the tennis court area, lunch again segregated, but from two until four everyone was allowed to mingle in the palm court. Dinner was again segregated in the cafeteria, then back to the dorms at dusk. Only communication with the outside world was strictly forbidden.

At first, the outside world didn't matter very much to Cindy so long as she could now see her parents. She first spotted them across the palm court and her beating heart sent out a message of love that drowned thought. "Cindy!" Her father scarcely had time to open his arms. She buried her face in his shoulder. "Oh, Dad, Dad." They stood there embracing and smiling for a long moment, their eyes wet with tears. Then she threw her arms around her mother. Marjory was the first to break away. Half-sobbing, half-laughing, she pushed back her hair with one hand and the other clung to Cindy's arm as though to reassure herself that her daughter was real and to make sure she would not vanish.

"I was so afraid I'd never see you again," Marjory said. "You shouldn't have been thrown in over there."

"It's all right, Mom, honestly."

"But all jumbled together. I've heard awful stories."

"Really, Mom, I've fixed up a corner very nicely."

"Have you been eating, Cindy?" her mother demanded.

"Like a horse, Mom."

"You look so thin. Doesn't she look thin, Howard?"

"I think she looks perfect," said the Ambassador, beaming. "The best thing I've seen in days."

With the relaxation of the hostages' confinement, exercise became a craze. Cindy would look out from the dorm window at the men below her on the tennis court. There was Kim, jogging around and around the courts, going through the motions of projecting an invisible javelin or discus. Colonel Anderson was leading a group of men in calisthenics, squatting hands on hips, "Ho!", leaping up, arms flying overhead to a point, down again on knees still tremulous, touching the ground, "Har!"

The day after, having talked late with her parents, Cindy was hurrying toward her dorm to make the curfew when she saw Kim. "I've missed you a whole lot," he said, and she agreed emphatically, but as soon as the words were out Cindy realized that she hadn't, not at all. She was relieved when the guards herded them back toward their respective dormitories.

In the freshmen women's dorm that night, Cindy began work that would sustain her in the weeks to come. Like Anne Frank, she would keep a diary. She began by noting the idiosyncrasies of her dorm mates: the sleepers, the readers, the card players, the ones who quarreled incessantly over a few inches of floor space. The game of Monopoly was a brief fad until one of the guards called it depraved and capitalistic and confiscated the dice. Gradually the mood relaxed.

> A few of the Saudi guards know English, and they like to kid us about gas in the States being up to eight dollars a gallon, things like that. But when they put a Ping-Pong table in the corridor I got even and trounced the lot of them, no mercy. It was really crazy how good it made me feel, that and hearing from one of the younger guards how upset he was missing school. Poor guy, as though this experiment in international togetherness was all our idea. God, what I wouldn't give for a room of my own.

Occupying more space in the journal than any other subject was the daytime rivalry between Kim and Salim. "Even if I weren't here I don't think they'd get on," Cindy jotted primly, adding a sample dialogue.

> "Actually, I don't know anything about cars." That's Kim in reply to Salim, who's mad for anything with wheels. "And you an American. How odd," from Salim. "I told you, I don't happen to fancy cars," Kim told him, sounding huffy but gleaming his teeth at Salim and saying to me as though he were frightfully bored, "Please, Cindy, talk to your friend and make him happy." Then Kim went into that gymnastic routine of his, hurling an imaginary shot put. If it had been real, I think he'd have sent it Salim's way.

Later, when she caught Kim alone, Cindy had said, "All I ask is, please try to be a little tactful, Kim. I mean, you don't strike me as even normally polite where Salim's concerned. I think it's dangerous, and I wish you'd stop."

"Listen," Kim had replied, "I may be outspoken, sometimes high-spirited, even occasionally boisterous, but never, never, tactless and impolite." Away went an imaginary javelin with a grunt of effort. "You see what bugs me is, I think that wog has fallen for you."

"Maybe he has. So what?"

"All I can say is, watch out," Kim warned her. "In this climate, people like that become a drag."

It was all becoming a drag. She was sick of the thick, syrupy coffee and longed for a cold glass of milk. She vowed never to eat lamb or rice again in her life. The TV was worse. The Embassy's stock of videotapes and discs had been confiscated and the one monitored local channel showed only Imans reading from the Koran, old newsreels of pilgrims in Mecca, and nothing current except wrestlers lathered in sweat. Aramco, which had its own station in Dhahran, wasn't broadcasting.

With the first days of March arrived the shamal, the spring wind, bringing sand and dust and heat from the desert. Flies buzzed everywhere since the air conditioning had failed. The sun was returning to his kingdom. Heat shimmered off the tennis courts, and nothing seemed to change except the weather, which got worse.

"I feel like I'm waiting in a station where the tracks have been torn up," Cindy wrote as one dazzling and molten day oozed into another, on and on without purpose. "But after all," she noted, "this is the mysterious East."

> MARCH 14TH. We are all getting ghastly ghetto-itis and we're all becoming dirty and smelly, too. My hair's so straight and icky I'm going to put it in a pigtail. If that doesn't work, I'll chop it off.

Cindy'd always made a fetish of being clean. She'd read once that it was a sign of madness to want everything clean. The plumbing wasn't working the way it should. Half the toilets were choked and there were insects everywhere. Sometimes she amused herself by counting the bites on her legs. "Bites, like fun. The flies here don't bite, they sting." She struck out "sting" and wrote "stab," adding, "and when a fly looks dead you can be pretty sure it's only carefully watching you while it works up an appetite."

On March 24th her first written word was "Bored! ! ! !" She wrote it over and over, perfecting her handwriting. Boredom was like pain. She woke with it, spent the day with it. Boredom loomed over her bed as she added with rococo scrollwork, "Flies proliferate." She tried to bolster her mood by assessing her good fortune.

> I have not been bitten by a mad dog. The building has not burned down with me inside. I have not been raped. My eyes have not been put out with red-hot pokers. So why am I complaining?

Outside, the muezzin gave the call to prayer, which jerked her away from the page. "For God's sake," she shouted, "won't somebody shut the damned window? It's giving me a headache."

"Odd," Cindy wrote reflectively after she had shut the window herself, "I seem to be becoming a four-letter-word person. Is it the boredom, or the fear behind the boredom?" Indeed, her entire nervous system seemed to be slipping out of control. That fine instrument which had been so obediently on call now twanged like a broken piano string at the slightest cause.

> APRIL FOOL'S DAY. How appropriate. Actually I'm feeling less like a fool than scared stiff. Nearly three months of school gone with me vegetating and scratching like a monkey. I've got to start studying something. Maybe I can sweet-talk Salim into letting us take out some books from the Embassy library.

> APRIL 4TH. Salim did it! The library's open for everybody. Not only that but, miracle of miracles, all restrictions are off from after breakfast until dinner. As long as we stick to the inner compound, the guards don't seem to give a

damn. Salim's taking credit, as usual, but just looking around you know there aren't as many guards as there used to be. Maybe they're being sent to the front, wherever that is. Anyway, three cheers.

APRIL 5TH. More good news. I have a pile of books, most of them on Saudi Arabia. Is there a chance I can figure out what makes them tick?

APRIL 7TH. Talk about women's lib. There isn't a single word in Arabic that means child, baby, infant—only boy on one side, girl on the other. By the way, another word for girl is "the incomplete one." Really nice. A girl's first smile means "please don't throw me out." About the only thing a girl can do while she grows up is worry about her "ird." The whole family worries about it, because deep inside, girls are supposed to be seething fires of sexuality. Just wink at a guy and that's it; no more "ird" or respectability and the whole family's disgraced forever. There's one out—they can put her to death. Talk about a dog's life. Please, God, let me out of this crazy zoo before I climb the walls.

A week later Cindy tried to amuse herself by testing her two Romeos on the subject of art. She didn't expect much from Salim. After all, representative art in Saudi Arabia hadn't progressed much beyond what she regarded as icky calendar art, Capri at sunset with voluptuous girls dangling grapes over half-opened mouths. The trap was baited with a number of her own sketches casually strewn about.

Salim arrived first. "They're frightful, aren't they?" she said, and Salim, who had been gazing at her the way every young girl wants to be looked at on occasion, replied in confusion, "Yes . . . no, I mean, they are very fine work, Cindy." Cindy, trying to be crafty and catch him out: "What do you make of this?" Not to be trapped, Salim replied, "I like it. I'm not sure what it is, but I like it, yes."

"It's a minaret."

"Really? Are they ever red?"

"Not that I know of, but that's how I paint them. I feel them that way."

Salim laughed nervously, trying to please. Then he smiled brightly, saying, "I would like very much to buy it." Surprised, Cindy told him she would think it over.

Kim proved another kind of philistine. He didn't try to hide it, he flaunted it. He didn't have to be encouraged to inspect the pictures, he simply pawed through them. He turned the one with the minaret upside down and asked, "What is this? Looks like the dog spilled its breakfast."

"How complimentary," Cindy said, though she knew he didn't mean it.

Finally Kim said, "I hate to admit it, but I like this. It's kind of shimmery and nice. When did you first get interested in painting?"

Cindy shrugged. "I guess it was one day when my dad took me to visit the British Museum. We were in London for a few days before he was posted to Norway, and he and Mom had just been on vacation in Greece. I remember asking him why all the Greek statues in the museum were broken, and Dad said—he's a philistine, too, for the record—'That's just how they are, old top. That's the way your Greek statues come these days.' "

"Your father said that?" Kim replied, and began to laugh as though it was the funniest thing he'd ever heard.

"Hey, if you don't quit that," Cindy told him, "you'll end up on the funny farm, committed by me."

"Don't say that! I'm not like my mother!" And he sounded so suddenly fierce that Cindy wondered if he were really worried about cracking up. If he was, the mood was quick to pass, and he grinned, saying, "Cancel that. I'll do anything to get my carcass out of this dump. Honest to God, Cindy, I mean it. What are we going to do? Hey, I'm talking to you."

"I was just thinking."

"A penny for 'em, Cindy girl."

"Oh, about counting bug bites, what else?"

Kim leaned toward her and lowered his voice almost to a whisper. "We'll be out of here soon. Take it from me."

"Kim, who are you kidding? We're here for good. We'll become a tourist attraction, the eighth wonder of the world."

"Damn right," he concurred, suddenly cheerful. "Once their oil runs out, they'll need us to bring in the bucks. 'General Aziz presents the Living Waxworks.' It may be tough for the first ten years, but we'll get used to it. No, don't worry, Cindy. We'll be gone long before that."

"I hope so," Cindy wrote the next day in her diary, "because the Embassy is falling apart." Except for the cooks, all that remained of the domestic staff were a few men flopping dirty mops around. Not that the Embassy was exclusive; the whole city of Riyadh was going down the tube.

> Example: no water pressure, so the pipes are hooked up to the municipal steam system. Result, flush the toilet and billows of steam. The electricity's off now more often than it's on.
>
> APRIL 16TH. Today we ladies of the freshman dorm struck a blow for privacy. While the guards watched we broke into the linen closet. We've been stringing sheets on clotheslines all day, making private compartments. At least we don't have to see each other lying in pools of sweat, and there's no more quarreling about who's trespassing on whose territory.
>
> APRIL 18TH. No breeze. Salim decided to supplement my reading with some revolutionary leaflets. I asked him if he

was trying to brainwash me and he said, with more spirit than I'm used to seeing him show, "Have we shut you up in a box, and kept you awake for hours? We are not ignorant savages. I thought these ideas might open your Western head, but never mind, I will take them away." I apologized for being so uptight, and I have read them. They weren't exactly as illuminating as Aladdin's lamp but they do show you there are two sides to this, which is easy to forget. For instance, one leaflet defined terrorism as the stationing of American troops overseas. Something to think about. Another one ended with a proverb: "I and my brother against my cousins; I and my cousins against the stranger." I suppose that also means me.

MAY 1ST. Jets over the city today. Distant explosions, but no explanations. Edith keeps rushing around with new rumors, but what's the use of listening? Nobody does any more, and poor Edith throws a fit.

MAY 3RD. I've spent most of today wondering about me. What will become of me? It's afternoon, and I ought to be in art class. Does school go on without me? Of course it does. I wonder who won the tennis cup this year. What I wouldn't give for a game of tennis. Last night I dreamed I was dead and buried. When I woke up I was so grateful to be breathing. I'm an awful coward. I don't want to die for ever so long. Life is marvelous. I never realized before how much I love life. If I get out of this mess I will never be quite the same person. Let them do anything just so I—that is, all of us—come out alive and with our faculties intact. Honestly, I am so curious about the future. What will I be in five years? Fifteen? My painting? The guy I'm going to marry? Where will we live? Some people say the world's losing its mind, going to pieces, but maybe it's waking up. There are all sorts of dangers but I don't want to miss any of it. I want to live through it all. Please.

That night, Cindy did something she hadn't done in years. She lay on her mattress and prayed. She didn't kneel, suspecting God had little use for grovelers. Then she rolled over face down on the pillow and cried without making a sound. "It's a nightmare, that's all. It's all just an awful nightmare."

The next morning the captivity took on a new and unexpected dimension. It began when Cindy wakened with the uncomfortable awareness that someone was looking at her. "You!" she said, sitting up with a start.

"Yes, me," said Kim, who sat in the guard's chair, the knees of his long legs flopping indolently apart like the wings of a weary butterfly.

"Why are you staring at me?"

"Oh," said Kim, "is it forbidden?"

"Have you been watching me all this time?" The idea was oddly unpleasant.

"For hours and hours," he said, "but with deep appreciation. Rest assured, you looked very pretty, like Sleeping Beauty."

"Where's the guard?" For an instant she had the wild hope that their captivity was over and that Kim had come to tell her they were free to go home.

"I throttled him, ever so quietly so's not to disturb you," Kim said. "I wish I had, but actually he's outside, watching them exercise. It's late, kiddo. Seen much of your wog friend?"

"Pardon?"

"Bin-Kabina."

"Oh, him."

"What do you mean, 'oh, him'? He's always hanging around. He's fallen for you."

"Can it, Kim. We've been over all that."

"It's just I wouldn't want you playing one of us off against the other," Kim said. "That's how wars get started."

"I thought wars were a bit more complicated than that."

"Don't forget the Trojan War," he said, then leaned forward with a happy smile on his handsome face. "Anyway, since nobody's around, I can tell you my surprise. I've got a radio."

"You've got to be kidding, Kim. How?"

"Remember how they rifled through the co-op?"

"That was weeks ago."

"No argument. But they dropped some stuff, including the radio. It was just there, I mean outside, in the bushes near the co-op door. The case was cracked, but it works. Now I've got it stashed away."

"I don't believe it," Cindy said, looking at him a little aslant, then laughing nervously. "You do mean it. Where?"

"Make yourself decent."

Within minutes they were casually strolling to the Embassy library. Cindy had books to return and Kim carried them for her. For the first time she noticed that his fingernails were freshly bitten back. A guard sat outside the entrance to the reading room, so at first they could talk only with their eyes. This part of the Embassy was so quiet that the stillness in the air, the guard, seemed to oppose their secret conspiracy. Kim led her to the back of the stacks. Bibles. Kim pulled one down off the shelf, saying, "I don't imagine the wogs have much use for this." Cindy was puzzled until he opened the book. Its pages had been scooped out, leaving a cavity for the small black-plastic cased transistor radio with an earplug on a slender white cord. "Two people can use this if they get their ears close together," Kim said as he replaced the Bible on the shelf with only the cord dangling down. "Listen, it should be the morning broadcast from London."

Cindy hadn't heard a newscast or seen an up-to-date paper for over three months, and in that time the world had effectively narrowed for her to a few acres. Nothing had substantially changed, only progressed and intensified. The Embassy and the struggle in Saudi Arabia must have been headline news once; now it was downgraded. "Our diplomatic correspondent reports that according to an informed source," chattered the disembodied little voice. She had managed to put so much out of her mind, and now it all came crowding back, a dismal parade of Job's messengers. The famine in India had deepened, radical military factions were threatening China with nuclear weapons if aid was not forthcoming. Food shortages were worldwide. Even the Soviet Union admitted slaughtering livestock because of the lack of grain reserves. In Poland the labor unions were rioting again and their unrest had spread to East Germany, where Soviet troops were breaking up the crowds. Additional massive Soviet troop movements in Hungary suggested an occupation of Yugoslavia might be contemplated. A stern protest was expected from the United States, where the President's popularity had sunk to a new low after he had pressured the Premier of South Africa to back down from his government's rejection of the United Nations' timetable for black majority rule. The U.S. Sixth Fleet had already arrived off Cape Town to avert any likelihood that the Soviet Indian Ocean flotilla might be drawn into the vacuum.

"Same old mess," Kim said.

"Only worse," Cindy despaired. "We'll be here forever, and there's not a thing we can do about it."

"Who knows. If there's a war, all bets are off."

"Why can't they let us go home before it's too late?" she lamented.

"Because they enjoy us so much, that's why. We're a sort

of international spittoon. But things'll work out. They always do."

"But how? If you play tennis, you don't just sit back and let the ball hit your racket because it's bound to come that way eventually."

"Hold on, Cindy, that's different. You're talking about something important. A game of tennis really matters."

"Oh shut up, you cynic."

"And you stop feeling sorry for yourself."

"Why shouldn't I feel sorry for myself? I am sorry for myself, and for all of us."

Kim put both hands on her shoulders. "Now listen to this. I'll only say it once." Kim was whispering. "We're getting out of here soon. I have it on good authority. We'll be rescued."

"Your dad?" she whispered back.

Kim returned a knowing smile but replied, "I've said my thing. Wait and see, but count on it." He held out his hand, which seemed to be overdoing it. "Okay? We'll see each other through this, come hell or high water."

"Why do you say that in such a silly voice?" she asked.

Kim shrugged. "Imagining high water in this place, I guess. Or maybe it's that pigtail of yours. It makes you look about ten years old. If I were the kid behind you in class . . ." He took hold of the thick plait, gave it a playful yank.

"Hey, cut it out, Kim. That hurts."

"Pax. Pax vobiscum," Kim pleaded, reverting to the vocabulary of Le Rosey. "You're much too ferocious for me."

"Thanks for letting me listen to the radio," Cindy relented.

"Well, if you appreciate it so much, how about being a

little nice to me for a change?" His wide blue eyes gazed straight into hers, so close she could feel his breath on her cheek.

"I'd like to be nice to . . . everybody," she said, looking away.

"It's so private here, Cindy. Don't you want to? If you don't want to . . ."

"I didn't say I didn't want to. Why not? If you want to, I'm psyched." But she wasn't. She was just bored and irritable.

"Do you mean it? Don't say it if you don't mean it. It's okay with me one way or the other. I mean, if I were to kiss you, would you have a spastic seizure or something?"

"Can't tell in advance."

"But something's on the tip of your tongue, I know you," Kim said, planting a trial kiss on the side of her throat without interrupting his commentary. "There. How did that go down?"

"What a talker you are," Cindy said, not elaborating that her response to him was more to boredom than to any of his self-confessed charm. Her overt reaction was to giggle. "Oh, dear."

Kim evidently did not take this amiss. He chuckled back and as he bore in, Cindy returned a passable imitation of real feeling, murmuring on surfacing, "Oh, Kim." She had tried to imagine falling for him, but in fact she felt herself turning stony in his embrace. In no way deterred, Kim presently went too far, too fast, with a dexterous right hand.

Cindy pulled away, with Kim laughing at the outraged look on her face. "There's more to you than meets the eye," he said.

"You're crude."

"Sorry, sorry," he placated her. "I'm just one of those

kids who always skips ahead to dessert. I'll take it easy. How about from the beginning?"

"You're asking for it," said Cindy, and was about to return his kiss when she became suddenly and horrifyingly aware of a pensive figure standing at the end of the row of shelves, not just any figure, either.

"Salim," she said aloud.

"Do I intrude," he said, not moving.

"As a matter of fact, old pal," Kim began, turning around languidly, one hand possessively on Cindy's shoulder.

"We were looking for books on Saudi Arabia," Cindy said quickly. "You know, under B for Bible Lands." She knew she was talking too much, too loudly.

"Yes, do join us in our quest," Kim relented. "How'd you know we were here, if I may ask?"

"When Miss Cindy wasn't in her dorm, or outside exercising, where else might she be?" Salim observed. "Besides, the guard outside has eyes, and ears."

The mention of ears put Cindy on alert. Was she only imagining it or did Salim's gaze impress some secret message into her? Did he know about the radio? The narrow cord still hung down from the shelf, conspicuously white, and she dared not encounter Salim's eyes.

Kim, too, must have received the message. He looked down at his feet, a muscle in his cheek moving. Then he raised his head and stared at Salim, angry and smiling. "Shall we have it out on the tennis court, bin-Kabina?" Kim asked. "What do you say, Black Beauty? Just rackets, mind, no balls."

"Cool it, Kim!" Cindy warned him. "Macho man, that's what you think you are, like some old Bronson film on TV."

Kim obligingly laughed, but it died on a false note. "You two go along," he said, suddenly magnanimous. "I want to browse among these sacred tomes." He gave Cindy a little push. "Go on, get some air. I'll see you later."

So she went with Salim, and if the radio was discovered or even suspected he made no mention of it.

"I should not have intruded," he began.

"Let's not go back to that, okay? You wanted to see me. How come?" Cindy asked.

"Because I like you, Cindy. Is that not enough?"

"Of course," she replied, noting that he had again dropped the "Miss," "that's a very nice reason."

"Also, I have found some American shampoo, Flex Balsam, so you will not have to wear your hair like a rope. You have very beautiful hair, like gold."

"Thank you. Thank you for the shampoo."

They were seated now by the tennis courts. Salim's manner was shy but his scrutiny was such that Cindy automatically crossed her legs. He was searching, searching for a common ground that was not there, a bond to build an association.

"Do you like the Bee Gees?" Salim asked. The question was so unexpected that Cindy laughed. "Are the Bee Gees amusing?" Salim asked, always very contained, very dignified.

"Oh, no, they're still quite popular back home." She didn't add, "among the older crowd."

"I have very many of their records and tapes. I could bring them over. And I have the music of the Crazed Maggots. Do you like them?"

"English, right? They're a little far out for me, but yes, I'd love to hear them. Maybe I'll change my mind."

"Today? I could bring them today?" He seemed to need to get away, collect himself.

"Whenever. I don't seem to be going anywhere."

And so their association began, listening to disco tunes, golden oldies that were passé back home and in Europe, and Cindy noted these encounters in her diary.

MAY 12TH. Salim brought more music. Today I met the Crazed Maggots. No comment, but Salim sat there entranced. And he confessed he was crazy about McDonald's and even Bagel Nosh. Where did he find that? And he'd eaten Smithfield ham somewhere and almost swooned with delight even though his soul may burn in hell.

MAY 14TH. Yet more music, again not entirely my bag, but Salim is really awfully good-looking in a dark and sinister way. Today I wondered what would happen if I touched him? We always sit on either side of the stereo. Would he scream "Unhand me" and bolt from the room?

MAY 15TH. I said, "You don't have to be so stiff. I won't panic if your sleeve brushes mine," and Salim didn't raise his eyes. He kind of wriggled his shoulders and spoke to one side, as though he were talking to a fellow prisoner. "Cindy," he said, "do you know what I am thinking about?" I told him no, how could I? I may have sounded a bit anxious. I know he's really uptight with me. It's hard to think of him as lots older than me, the way he acts, but I guess he's had hardly any exposure to girls. It has to be tough being a boy here, almost as tough as being a girl. Well, then he told me what he was thinking of. He said, "I'm thinking about seeing you in the window that night, in a blaze of light for all the world to see, like an angel, and only I was there." This looked like trouble. I knew it was Christmas time he was talking about. For me it was a long time ago, but he made it sound like yesterday. "You are very beautiful," he said, but he wouldn't look at me. "Come on," I said, "I look a mess. What are you talking about?" Now things got just a weeny bit intense. "I said you are beautiful, that is what I am talking about. I'm so glad your hair is free again." He was staring right at me in this solemn way and I kind of laughed, and so things wouldn't build up I said, "Gee, that's really nice of you, Salim." That may have slowed him down, but he smiled anyway. He has a smile that lights up his whole face. It's like when a dark pool is touched by the sun.

MAY 17TH. Should I be flirting with Salim, or shouldn't I? Yesterday I gave him sort of a flirty look, and he didn't blush the way he used to. Am I walking into trouble? If I am, I can't help it. Everything's a bore or frightening, like Kim's radio. We were passing records around today and our hands accidentally touched. Salim couldn't have been more startled if he'd gotten an electric shock.

MAY 18TH. The radio says such horrible things I hate to listen. The only good thing now is flirting with Salim. Am I only using him? I asked for some art supplies yesterday and he said he'd see what he could do. I know it isn't easy, even if the city isn't surrounded by the King's forces, which is what most of us believe and Salim isn't admitting. Most of the shops are closed, he tells me. Now that it's so hot, I mentioned the pool, too. Couldn't it be filled again? Really, I'm awful. I got up and stood right in front of him and put my hands on his shoulders. I think I could draw the soul out of that poor guy. Of course he said he'd try, and I stepped back and clapped my hands for joy, cutsie-poo. God, what a game. I even blew him a kiss and he said, "Excuse me," so I blew him another. He looked terribly uncomfortable. But I wonder, might he take advantage, or is he too inhibited? I think he's even forgiven my friendship with Kim—it's just a little embarrassment between us. And yet today, something odd happened. It was a very piggy day and I was sweating, and suddenly Salim reached out, touched my forehead with his finger, and then put his finger to his lips, saying, "Dew of Cindy." How about that? I hope this diary makes it through. It just may get a bit Scheherazade-ish. And what would Kim have done, if he'd been around? I really don't want them hating each other.

Cindy lay asleep, her fists clenched on either side. In her dream she saw Salim robed in white and gold, the Sheikh of Araby. He was not alone. There was the rest of the Embassy staff, ranged around the wall of the reception room, except that they weren't really Salim or Kim or the members of the staff, but camels dressed up in disguise, and they were talking about Cindy in very clinical terms. "Overwhelming stress," and "hysterical neurosis, dissociative type." One camel leaned very close, asked, "Does she suffer?" and another, sounding rather like Doctor Harper, replied, "No, not much. Withdrawal is a complete rejection of reality. It's not painful, since it's a kind of psychic death." The camels hovered, becoming more human in form. "Either her mind will digest the past or it won't," said the first camel.

"What do you imply by 'won't'?"

"That it's quite possible she may retreat into psychic disintegration."

"Permanently?"

"That's possible, if we push too hard."

"There must be some pressure."

Cindy looked out from slitted lids. The desert compressed into blank white walls. The camels became men in uniforms just outside the open door. She was back in her hospital bed.

"What do you suggest? We no longer have the rack at our disposal."

"Simply do your utmost, Doctor Harper."

"Short of pushing her over the brink into total madness, I'll do what I can."

"Keep the time factor in mind," said the stranger. "We're concerned here with a great deal more than one person's sanity."

9

Doctor Harper stared down at her. He looked tired and distracted, even defeated. "You're awake in there, aren't you, Cindy?" he said softly, as if hoping he was wrong. "I know you are. I suppose you heard everything."

Cindy felt oddly sorry for the doctor, who seemed sometimes so like her father. He was her only link with the world. She dared not lose him, so she moaned, let her lids flutter, then opened her eyes, saying, "Oh, did you say something, Doctor? I suppose you want to turn on the machine." He looked at her quizzically, then let it pass.

"It's not a matter of want, Cindy. We've been talking on and off now for the better part of three days. I'd like three weeks for you to decompress; better still, three months. That's what you deserve, but we're outranked, you and I. We're under pressure to come up with something soon. Let's help one another," he explained before activating the tape recorder, at which point he went on more formally, "We were talking about the captivity. I want to move on to the execution if you're up to it, but one or two things first. You say they didn't try brainwashing."

"Only leaflets."

"No pressure?"

"No, not really."

"And you gradually had more freedom?"

"Yes," Cindy said. "There seemed to be fewer and fewer guards. We suspected they were needed for the fighting. As long as we got back to our own dorms at night, and didn't try to get out, they didn't seem to give a damn what we did."

"They even refilled the pool?"

Cindy nodded. She remembered Kim making circular commotions in the water, splashing and snorting. For a few days it had been almost like a resort, and she'd been able to imagine that the robed men who prowled about as they swam were not captors but protectors. This mood had not lasted long. Some of the regular guards had been replaced by older men who stared at the bathers as though they were depraved in their seminakedness, and sometimes they would sight down their guns at the swimmers as though about to indulge in casual target practice. By then, algae had gotten into the water, its surface was a green carpet, and no fresh water was to be spared.

"So you stopped swimming," Doctor Harper said.

"We did after we heard that the new guards were using the pool as a urinal. Anyway, I needed to spend more time with my parents, especially Mom."

"She was depressed, I take it. Was she drinking?"

"Oh, no, they'd smashed all the bottles. I'm not a psychiatrist but, well, just the way she looked," Cindy explained, remembering those guileless, suffering smiles and those eyes, dog's eyes, retriever's eyes, pointing mournfully toward New England.

Cindy had always thought of her mother as a bristler and a fighter, but then all Marjory had done was moan, "I've always been a leaf tossed about the world, and now look where I'm putting down roots. Oh, how funny, isn't this funny?" Her laughter had been close to tears. "And do you know what a little bird told me? 'You wouldn't want little Cindy marrying an Arab, would you?' And I said, 'Heaven forbid, she's much too young.' " She was making it into a joke, but her eyes pleaded, tell me it isn't so. And Cindy had said, "Mom, I presume that little birdie was Kim Anderson, and he is sometimes a real nurd." "I'm so glad," Marjory had confided. Her fingers, damp and hot like worms, had closed over Cindy's hand. "It's just there's so much to worry about, dear, and I'm not feeling awfully well."

"Was your mother ill?" Doctor Harper interjected.

"Mom thought she had cancer," Cindy explained. "She didn't tell me that, Dad did. It had happened once before. The first time she'd convinced everyone, and they were ready for exploratory surgery. Dad told me it was just nerves, and not to worry."

"Poor Marjory," Howard Cooper had said to his daughter, "she hates all this so. She can still make me feel like Hannibal crossing the Alps, but I'd let her go if I could."

"And how was your father holding up?" asked Doctor Harper.

"Just great," Cindy replied.

Howard Cooper was a refuge and always would be. Cindy remembered him lugging her into his arms where she rocked sadly against his chest. "Don't listen to rumors," he said. "That's why your mom has a nervous stomach. The first rumor says, if X happens we're doomed. The next rumor says, if X doesn't happen, that's the end of the human race. We're damned either way, but don't bet on it, kiddo. Things work out. I don't exactly know why, but I've got a conviction that there's something about the human race. We blow ourselves up ten times, and we're back again in the burning zone like some desert plant you can't uproot. So hang in there, and we'll make it, even with incompetents like me running things."

At this she'd whispered back, "Dad, don't talk that way. You're a great Ambassador." He'd studied her face carefully for any trace of patronage. Evidently satisfied, he'd said quietly, "I ought to wish you back at school on a magic carpet." Cindy hadn't reminded him that summer vacation would already have begun. "But Lord knows, it's been a comfort having you here." It was then, despite a pledge of absolute silence, that Cindy had told her father about the radio.

"Doctor Harper," Cindy said, interrupting her recollections, "if I could only walk a bit, on deck or even in a hallway."

"That doesn't seem unreasonable. I'll have to get an official clearance, but yes, I think I can arrange that."

"What you're really saying is no."

"Not at all. If you were awake a while back you should realize I'm not the final authority around here. Not even, necessarily, where your treatment is concerned."

"I may know what you're talking about, Doctor, but I don't know what it all means. Do they want to torture me for information?"

"Good Lord, Cindy, hardly torture." The doctor looked sad, as though he'd been caught out in a lie.

"I think I have the right to know why I'm here, Doctor. But I've given up on that. All I'm asking for is some fresh air. You can blindfold me and stick my head out of a porthole."

"There aren't any, Cindy."

"Then on deck, just for a minute. Please?"

"I'd like nothing better than to conduct this interview in a couple of deck chairs with a steward serving tea and little cakes."

"The air is so weird. It's like an airplane," she interrupted.

"Tea and little cakes," the doctor repeated, "but apart from this being a navy ship on extended duty, you wouldn't enjoy the deck. We'd have all sorts of problems."

"It sounds like . . ." Cindy began.

"Like what?"

"Nothing."

"Come on, Cindy." Doctor Harper laughed out loud. "I think my young Sherlock Holmes has made a deduction; am I right?" Cindy didn't deny it. "That the deck is very wet? That, in fact, we are aboard a submarine, a very modern and well-equipped submarine, but still, as they used to say, a 'pig boat.' Well, you're quite right, and if my guess is correct we're sitting on the bottom, say a hundred yards down." Superficially, Cindy was stunned, yet deep inside she had been entertaining the possibility for some time. "So, Cindy, if that's settled, I'll be glad to refresh your recollection up until the time of the killing. Are there any blocks now?"

"Not that I'm aware of, Doctor."

"What about a rescue attempt? I mean, beyond mere gossip. Did that seem likely?"

"Kim and even Salim brought it up, but I don't know how seriously. Maybe they were competing in a way."

"We're talking about late June," Doctor Harper said, as much for the tape recorder as for Cindy.

"I think so. It was terribly hot."

Day had followed day in that dateless calendar of waiting. Each cool night had gently rolled over into another sun-drenched and sweltering day. Cindy had written in her diary on June 26th, "The sun is like a lion, roaring out of the desert. The Saudis are always up at first light, shouting 'Rise and pray, rise and pray!' "

Prayers followed by sweat, that was the sequence. Her clothes had begun to rot from perspiration. She had prickly heat and her nose suffered worst of all from the dust. But worse than the dust, the heat, and the flies was the tedium of waiting, with fear always buried just below the surface. The little hidden radio offered its constant alarms of mounting world crisis. Then both Kim and Salim came with surprises.

> JUNE 30TH. Today I met a brand-new Kim. I don't suppose I'll get to know this one, but I think I could like him a lot. I don't know what got him started, maybe he and his father had been at each other, but he said sort of out of the blue, 'You know, my mom really doted on me. I guess Dad must have been jealous as hell.'

"When you were little?" Cindy asked him.

"Yeah. It must have been tough on him, coming back from special assignment only to get it in the neck when he got home. I was really scared of him, isn't that weird? God, the way they fought at night, and I'd be in bed, listening, wishing he'd go off again and not come back. I'd get so scared sometimes I could hardly breathe."

"You sound a little funny right now," Cindy told him.

"I used to have asthma, but I've mastered it."

"Listen, Kim, you don't have to talk about it to me if you don't want to."

"I don't, much, but I'm going to if you don't mind. I guess I've had all this time to think and nobody to tell. You know, it's funny, but it's not easy for me to look you in the face."

"You needn't be afraid of what you'll see," Cindy said.

"It's what you'll see that worries me. You see, I used to think what happened to Mom was his fault, the way their marriage went sour, but that wasn't the problem at all. It was there all the time, in the blood."

"I'm not sure I follow, Kim." Cindy was attentive now, knowing her help was needed.

"Mom's condition was, well, congenital. I might be . . . might end up like her. Sometimes I think . . . I don't know. . . ." His voice trailed off.

"Kim, that's ridiculous! You're the last person on earth . . . I mean it," Cindy insisted, putting more astonishment into her voice than she felt.

Two days later the chink in the armor had closed. The old Kim came around early, saying, "Pssst! How're things at Alcatraz?" Very confidential then, as though speaking through an air duct to the prisoner next door, "You know, sweetheart," trying to sound like Humphrey Bogart, "at this hour you're not such a hot-looking chick." Cindy told him that he could get the hell out, but he kept sniffing around like a dog on a scent.

"Where'd you get that?" he suddenly accused, pointing at her neck.

"This?" She touched the gold locket she wore. "I've had it for years, for heaven's sake. It was Mom's."

"He gives you things."

"What?"

"Like pencils and paper."

"Big deal. What's so wrong with that?"

"I'll tell you what's so wrong . . ." and then glancing up, "well, speak of the devil. Look who's here. Come on in, Black Beauty. What can we do for you?" The two young men stared at each other like hostile dogs.

As though to refute that vulnerable side that he had so recently revealed, Kim was deliberately probing for a place to hurt, and Cindy knew it. "Kim, please don't start in," she warned.

"Listen," he shot back, "when I'm conversing with Mohammed, I don't need to hear from Allah." Not bad, he grinned sardonically, but if his mind groped for something that would put the "miserable little wog" in his place and thus demonstrate the triumph of Western intellect, it eluded him. The smile became as empty as a Disney rodent's, then died entirely. Nothing had come.

"I see you are busy now, Cindy. I'll come back later," Salim offered, as if Kim were not there.

"Don't. Don't be a bad sport. Hey, Black Beauty!" Kim spoke to an empty doorway, then rounded on Cindy. "Well, he seems to know when he's not wanted."

"Whose room is this?" she said. Two of the secretaries were there with nothing better to do than listen.

"May I generalize?" Kim asked, his voice up a decibel or two.

"Keep it down," she told him, "and if you want to know, you're becoming a royal pain in the butt, Kim Anderson."

"You are one maddening tease," he grinned back.

"Whatever you're going to say, Kim, say it out in the hall," she insisted, getting ready to leave the room. "There are ladies present."

In the corridor they paced up and down. "I've made a bit of a study," said Kim, "and do you know, for instance, they've got the lowest national intelligence quotient in the world?"

"I don't need to hear this, Kim. I mean it."

"Seriously, they're neither black nor white. Their blood's completely gone to seed. If you want confirmation, ask my father. He knows. They're stupid, and they're mean, like those shiny black bugs that sting. They get their stingers into you, and you smash 'em, and still they go on stinging for no reason. That's what the wogs are like."

"Very instructive," Cindy replied caustically, "and now that we've heard from your father, what does your mother have to say?"

The impact of her words on Kim was almost physical. He seemed to stiffen as though absorbing a fist to the mid-section, then turned away, gazing out over the tennis courts. "That's a bit of a low blow," he said at last.

"Tit for tat," said Cindy, who wasn't ready to let up. "And while I'm on the subject of stupid and mean, why did you go around and put a bee in Mom's bonnet about me joining a harem?"

"What?" Kim turned on her.

"Don't act so innocent. You know what I mean."

"Oh, that." Kim lowered his eyes. "All right, so I'm a nerd sometimes. I don't really know anything about their national IQ, okay? All I know is, they've got us locked up here, and somebody I'm damned fond of is taking bribes from a guard."

"I never thought of it like that," said Cindy, and she hadn't. She began to feel the guilty party.

"You won't let it make any difference between us, will you, Cindy? Not even when we get out of here?"

"That'll be the day." Cindy had lately come to accept imprisonment as an eternal state.

"We'll be out soon, that's a promise. Really. So, how about a kiss to seal the bargain?"

"Sure, why not," Cindy replied, trying for enthusiasm. "And listen, Kim, I'm sorry, too."

Kim folded his arms around her. "You're outrageously pretty," he whispered. Cindy closed her eyes. Anything was better than arguing, and necking with Kim did not seem a serious business. She had a feeling he would have done the same with any girl who was handy and willing.

"Actually," she wrote later in her diary, "I'm not really sure he has that much use for girls. He just likes showing off, like a peacock." Sometimes Kim was rough, but he was never dangerous. When she said no, he stopped. Cindy found Salim, who had scarcely touched her, far more electric and disturbing.

She was staring out of the window, watching Kim go through his discus-throwing routine, when Salim returned.

"What do you see, Cindy?"

"Nothing," she said, turning away from the window. "Just bored. Can you understand that?" Salim nodded, holding out a plastic bag. "Goodies for me? Good goodies?" She tried to sound excited in a mindless way that she supposed Arabs found charming. The bag was full of tubes of oil paint. "Salim, this must have cost you a fortune."

"It's nothing."

"I can't take all this," Cindy said, remembering what Kim had said about taking bribes from a guard.

"Sell me a painting, then."

"You can take what you like."

Together they went through the portfolio. "These roses, they have the color of unripe almonds," he said. "And what is this?"

"I'm entering my Van Gogh period. It's a night sky. No, turn it the other way."

"To me it is a nuclear explosion." Salim held up another painting. "And this?"

"It's an arm, silly. It's not finished. I must have done it in my sleep, it's so good. I mean, isn't it really armish? It'll flex for you, shake hands, wrestle, whatever."

"If you like it best," he said gravely, "I will take it."

"You should take what *you* like best."

Salim put the painting of the arm aside, saying, "May I talk to you, Cindy?"

It sounded serious. "Sit down," she said.

"You are very beautiful," Salim informed her.

"Yes, I know. I wish you'd tell me something I'm not sure of, Salim, like what a great artist I am."

"As far as I am concerned, Cindy, you are. I like so much to watch you paint. I would like very much to hold something the way you hold your paintbrush. Such tenderness. That, Cindy, is how I would like to hold you."

"Salim," Cindy said, standing up, "I'm afraid Kim will be coming back any minute."

"I do not fear that one, only what I might do to him. There is a saying among my people, that the shared kettle does not boil."

"Will you explain that? . . . No, don't bother." She knew very well that he wanted to kiss her but dared not. Cindy half-wanted him to try, but that would be one more complication in her life that she would be wise to avoid. "The paints are marvelous," she said, edging him toward the door. "I love them. Next time I'll paint you a leg, one you can kick with." That clearly wasn't what Salim wanted, but dutifully he went, and when he was gone, only then did Cindy begin to breathe freely again.

JULY 7TH. Thank goodness, it looks as though Kim and Salim have worked out a calendar. At least they don't butt heads here anymore. Still, I'm afraid I've made them enemies. They're like a couple of bombs ticking away, acting like perfectly normal clocks. I hope they never explode.

The next day began badly and got worse. Cindy awoke to the sound of distant gunfire. Edith reported it was the Bedouin attacking the suburbs. Then the guards began stringing wire outside. Edith announced they were mining the Embassy for a suicidal last stand, a Saudi Arabian version of the Alamo. Then soap was handed out and it was revealed that the wires were for stringing laundry. Everyone began scrubbing with a will. Cindy hadn't seen her mother in a better mood for weeks. It wasn't to last. Before everything could be hung to dry they were prodded back into their quarters and told if they ventured outside they'd be shot. Not even Edith offered an explanation, and it remained for a grim-faced Salim to bring the news. One of the guards assigned to the bachelors' dorm had fallen from the roof and broken his neck. Accident or murder? There were rumors that the broken neck came first, then the fall. Salim had been on that roof and he considered the railing there too high to permit such an accident. By dinnertime any doubts had been resolved. While the prisoners ate in an odd sort of reverential silence, there was nothing to hear but the thud of hammers. Posters were being nailed up.

The hastily written message was brief and ominous: "Americans: There is no time to waste. The murderer must admit his guilt and confess his crime within the next twelve hours or the consequences will be severe." What consequences? Cindy wondered. It was always hard to be sure with the Saudis. Sometimes they contented themselves with terrible threats and were very lenient, leaving the real punishment to Allah. "May Allah send a high wave and wash him from the world." Perhaps they would leave it at that.

On the other hand, perhaps they meant to set an example, even if doing so would give the United States an excuse to retaliate.

To predict their actions according to Western formulas was of little use, Cindy supposed, and when she ran into Kim on the way back to the dorm, he could only repeat one of his father's stories about the scorpion who asked a frog for a ride across the River Nile. The frog declined, suspecting that the scorpion would sting him if he complied. This the scorpion denied, since he could not swim and would die as well. That made sense to the frog and they had reached midstream before the scorpion reverted to his natural instincts. The expiring frog murmured with his last strength, "Why did you do that? Now you will drown." And the scorpion replied sadly, "I know, but remember, dear friend, this is the Middle East."

The next morning resolved any doubts as to how the Saudis meant to deal with the situation. Cindy and the other prisoners were called outside to the palm court. Half-suspecting he might have been killed in battle, she was surprised to see General Aziz there. It hadn't been all that long since she had thought of him as the bird man, but if he was a bird still, it was a vulture. He must have lost weight and had very little sleep, for he didn't so much look older as he looked more frightening. He began to speak, and he was frightening to hear, not cruel for cruelty's sake as in the stories about him, but impersonal, a force for justice doing what had to be done even though no one, not even himself, wanted it that way.

"There are times for silk," he said, "and times for sand-paper. You Americans may think the world was created for your personal comfort, but in this country we have a law, *sharia*. It treats all men the same, and for each crime there is an equal punishment. Blood for blood!" As his speech went on, it became clear that he was not so much concerned with the actual guilt or innocence of any individual as with the necessity of returning an eye for an eye. One Saudi citizen was dead. Some American had killed him, and therefore one American must die. Preferably, but not necessarily, the murderer.

No one said a word. Then Cindy saw her father stepping forward out of the crowd. For the first time in his life Howard Cooper appeared to have forgotten to shave. Still, he looked so tall and calm that she could have cried if she hadn't been too petrified to make a sound. She expected a protest or argument from him, then realized he was offering himself as the victim. If General Aziz insisted on blood revenge, then he would submit on behalf of the others in the Embassy. Cindy felt a scream expanding inside her and then General Aziz had his arm around the Ambassador's shoulder. They talked confidentially for a few moments, and her father walked away.

Then General Aziz explained that, good as the Ambassador had been to offer himself, only possible suspects would be considered. To that extent they would help Allah choose. Seven names were on the list, he said, seven men all housed in the building where the death had occurred. These seven were hurried forward, and a drawing of straws took place. As Cindy watched with horrified fascination, six of the American men rejoined the crowd. One remained, holding the short straw.

"If I had ten thousand lives," he was saying, "I would cheerfully lay them all down for the good of my country." It was Colonel Anderson. General Aziz leaned forward, said something Cindy couldn't hear, and then Colonel Anderson went on, "No, I have nothing to add to that statement." He didn't seem to show any fear, except that just as the guards took hold of him to lead him away he seemed to wink, no normal wink but a sort of convulsion of his whole face. It was ghastly.

Within a few minutes Kim had broken through the milling crowd, crying, "Cindy! Cindy!" and she couldn't help echoing back, "Yes! Yes!" because she felt his dread. He was so upset he could hardly make sense. She could feel his poor brain darting this way and that for some means of saving his father. The only hope seemed to be Salim, if he could, and would, intercede. Salim would never listen to Kim, so she would have to try.

"Cindy," Salim said when she asked him, "you know I would do anything I could for you. But this . . . Cindy, this is not like asking for a fresh tube of paints. This is Insh' Allah, the will of God."

"But he's not even guilty," she pleaded. "He's an innocent man."

"Perhaps, Cindy. Perhaps not. But there must be an example made, before the world."

"You could at least try!" she told him, half-crying. "You could speak to the General."

"Yes, I could speak to him, Cindy, as your father has done, but not even General Aziz could change things now, not even if he knew your nuclear missiles would be turned against us. Colonel Anderson is a dead man. It is better to think of him that way."

Thinking was one thing, but feeling was another, and Cindy kept trying, knowing it was hopeless. Kim just then burst into the room, as if he had been listening outside. His face was wild, and he looked ready to attack Salim with his bare hands even though Salim had his gun slung over his shoulder. "For the love of God," he pleaded, "my father hasn't killed anyone. You know that."

"That is for Allah alone to know. I do not like that one of ours is dead, or that one of yours must die, but permit me to speak plainly. Though we are not friends, I regret this. And yet you must know, as I know, that your father is a spy." Salim was very calm and quiet.

"He is not! He is not a spy!" Kim denied vehemently.

More to Cindy than to Kim, Salim said with sad weariness, "He is, you know. We could trap spiders in the plans he spins."

"But what has that to do with murder?" Cindy pleaded.

"It is God's will, not mine," said Salim, and left the room.

Kim didn't move to follow him. His feet might have been set in cement.

Cindy hesitated, afraid to leave Kim, then ran out into the corridor. Salim was nearly at the stairs when she caught up with him. "When does the . . . the execution take place?" she asked, out of breath.

"Tomorrow," Salim said. "At dawn. Of course we are not always on time, as you know. We are not as efficient as you Americans."

JULY 10TH. Nothing will be the same after today. I want to forget what happened, but if this diary will ever matter I have to put it down. Last night it was never quiet.

Beyond the Embassy walls the city murmured unceasingly, as if it knew, and in the compound a clanking and banging went on until the sky turned crystal green and the muezzin began his call. No one had been able to sleep, and when the sun burned red once again through the windows, the prisoners began to wonder if it was perhaps a hoax, like the mock firing squad they'd paraded before the hostages in Tehran eight years before.

Rumors flew back and forth but it was only a delay in setting up the television equipment. Saudi justice was to be dramatized for the world. The sun rose overhead, and heat shimmered on the tennis courts. The palms hung limp and dusty. Finally the cameras were in place, and General Aziz appeared.

> The General said the men would have to witness the punishment, as he called it. He didn't force the women to come but most of us were out there anyway. I couldn't find Kim, or I'd have tried to be with him. Edith said Colonel Anderson had been locked up overnight in one of the code rooms. I don't know how she knew. When two guards brought him out, his legs stopped working before he got to the tennis court. Then he fell down, and he put his arms around one of the guard's ankles. It looked as if he was begging for his life. I was so sorry for Kim. His father wasn't on the ground for very long before they hauled him up by his handcuffs. The steel flashed like fire. They'd dug a hole in the tennis court, and next to it they stopped and pushed Colonel Anderson down until he was kneeling. His head came up only once. It wasn't just pale, but gray, no color at all, like it was stamped out of old tin. He didn't shout anything about God bless America. I guess I thought he would. He just kept saying, "Oh, Mother." Just "Oh, Mother," over and over. I thought I was going to be sick and I wanted to leave and go back to the dorm, but the guards wouldn't let anyone move. The executioner was a huge man in a long white robe. He pushed the sleeve back before he pulled out a long curved sword. General Aziz raised his hand in a signal and then the guards leaned away from Colonel Anderson. Somebody did something, pricked him in the side maybe, to make Kim's dad straighten up. When he did, he yelled "Oh, Mother" again and then the sword flashed and I

couldn't watch anymore. They buried him there in the hole in the tennis court.

Cindy was shaken and crying but she knew she had to help Kim. She looked for him, but met her father first. Neither said a word, but clung together as if a fierce wind were blowing. Finally the Ambassador said, "He's in the library. I was just going to him. If you think you're up to it, sweetheart, you might be more appreciated." Cindy nodded, wondering if any words could be the right ones for Kim just then.

"But what do I say to him? It's okay, your dad has nothing to fear anymore? Or tell him his father's a hero who's given his life for his country?" She was crying again.

Howard Cooper hugged his daughter, then gave her a gentle push in the direction of the library. She knew she had to go, as much for her own sake as for Kim's, and only hoped she wouldn't make it worse for him.

> Kim was sitting there at one of the reading tables. When he heard me coming he looked up, and his face was the worst thing I've ever seen. He was trying to hold his mind and his body together, and it showed. I don't think he even recognized me, because when I put my hand on his shoulder he jumped, as if I were a snake or something. All I could think of to say was how sorry I was. Then Kim said, "I was just getting to know him. After all these years, I was just getting to know him." Then he put his head down on the table and said how tired he was. I think he wanted to go to sleep, to blot it all out. I didn't know what to do so I just sat there. After a while he said, not looking at me, "I don't want your pity. Leave me alone, will you!" "Only if you're okay," I said. "I'll be fine," he said and thumped his fist down on the table. "I'll be fine, damn it!" So I went, not knowing if I should have left him or if I'd done something wrong. He didn't look fine, and I felt like a coward leaving him.

Back at the dorm, everyone was talking about what would happen next. Would they be locked in again? Would the U.S. retaliate, and if so, how? And would the King's National Guard ever break through to the city? And none of it seemed to matter to Cindy as much as Kim sitting alone in the library, hating the world and wishing he'd never been born.

> When Salim turned up later on, I didn't want anything to do with him and said some words that used to shock me. I know they shocked him. "Cindy, please do not speak like that," he said, and I said them all over, screamed them, and Salim stood there with his head turned away as though I had hit him.
>
> Then he asked if we could go outside to talk. I went as far as the corridor, and told him if he had anything to say to spit it out and leave me alone. "I wish I did not have to speak of what happened," he said. "But you feel compelled to," I answered. "You killed Kim's father and now you come to me begging for forgiveness." I knew that wasn't entirely fair. "This is war," Salim said. "That was a consequence of war." I told him I never wanted to see him again and he said, "Here is my right arm. Take a knife and cut it off. I will be grateful, if it will make everything good between us." I was so angry I couldn't even laugh. "Cindy, please," he went on. "We Arabs, our hearts do the work of our brains, and at heart I am a pacifist." I yelled at him that he was a liar. "You with that great big gun on your back! You don't know what the truth is!"

Cindy was trembling with rage, and to calm herself began to pace up and down the corridor.

"I have never fired a gun, Cindy. For me, it is as alien as . . . as a fishing pole."

She almost laughed at that. "And we're the fish, I suppose," remembering General Aziz's story, "in a barrel."

"No, please, Cindy. I'm more on your side than you

think. I do not hate Americans, as some do." Then he came out with it, as though the secret no longer mattered. "I know about the radio, but I have not reported it. If things go badly, I will save you." Cindy said nothing, staring stony-eyed down at the pile of dirt and rubble on the tennis court that was Anderson's grave. "Listen, my name is bin-Kabina —that means, son of Kabina. Kabina was my mother. One is usually named after one's father but I am a Rashid. We are different, an old desert tribe, descendants of Ishmael. He is in your Bible. If things go badly, I will take you safe to my tribe. They know the desert, what your maps call 'The Empty Quarter,' like no other people. I will take you safe there or die trying, Cindy."

"I don't want any more people dying," she said. "You can't make up for what happened that way. You don't bury one corpse under another. Now leave me alone, Salim."

The muezzin began yodeling from his minaret and Salim, who seemed to have run out of steam, asked me if he could pray first. That was his business, so I just shrugged. He knelt down with his forehead touching the floor, repeating the formula. When it was over he let out his breath with a sort of hiss, as if he were relieved, and drew his hands down over his face. That's supposed to help absorb the blessing from the prayer. When he stood up he said something really embarrassing. "Cindy, for me, you are as beautiful as Allah. I know that is a sin to say, but you are for me so fair, like the inside of a seashell, like a pearl."

I was still feeling awful, so I said sarcastically, "Thanks. If it weren't for you I would be on a beach somewhere. I'd be as brown as a nut or maybe red as a tomato." He asked me not to joke. "You think I'm joking? That's how far apart we are," and I went into the bathroom marked LADIES and closed the door. I knew he wasn't ready to follow me in there, not yet, anyway.

10

"Before we get down to business," Doctor Harper asked, "will you eat something? You should be hungry, Cindy."

"Sure, from all the exercise I'm getting. I don't suppose there's a tennis court on this sub."

"There is a small gym. I could speak to the captain, but you've got to build yourself up before you're ready for that, let alone tennis," the doctor said, settling a tray before her. Obligingly, Cindy began to eat. "I hear you're quite a tennis player," Harper continued. "Well, we'll get you back on the court in no time. I've never played myself. Racquetball's my game, when I have the time. I suppose you have some favorite pros?"

"Sure, I've always gone for the Fanning sisters," Cindy said. "The way the twins Val and Liz took the doubles in the U.S. Open."

"Yeah, they're sensational," the doctor agreed absently. "Did you see Pam Fanning in the Wimbledon finals?" she asked.

"Best match since Borg and McEnroe," Harper said. "Now don't forget to eat."

"No, I won't," Cindy replied. Pam Fanning was famous, all right, but not for tennis. She'd won the New York and Boston marathons in '86 and '87. It was possible that Doctor

Harper had agreed just to make her eat, but had he deliberately lied to gain her confidence?

"Cindy, what's the matter? Did I say something wrong?"

"No, nothing," she said, hastily taking another bite.

"Well, look, I'd love to talk about it with you but I'm really not that much of a tennis buff. You finish that food. I don't want you to wear yourself out. We need some of that excess energy to wind this up." He gestured toward the tape recorder. "It may be a strain."

"Right now?" There were dark places she felt unable to explore.

"Say, within the next few hours." Cindy nodded her assent. Harper held the microphone in her direction, turned up the volume control. "Now here we go. Tell me, Cindy, was there any feedback regarding Colonel Anderson's execution that you were aware of at the Embassy?"

"Some," Cindy replied cautiously, on guard now not only against the black terrors of recollection but against betrayal, of what and to whom she did not know. Maybe Harper had made an inadvertent slip, but what if he had lied? It was so trivial, really. Perhaps she was becoming totally paranoid, but the fabric of trust was torn and the misunderstanding about the Fanning sisters had loosed suspicions she had previously kept in check.

"The media turned him into something of a martyr," said Doctor Harper. "There were reports that he forgave the executioner, kissed an Arab child. Believe me, back home there was a real surge of public opinion calling for revenge."

"We heard, over the radio," Cindy admitted. The BBC overseas service reported speculation about U.S. intervention to assist the King, and the Soviet Union was offering at least verbal support to the rebels. Both superpowers accused the other of actually sending military supplies and advisers.

Both denied the accusations which, according to the BBC, were equally true. It had seemed to Cindy and the others that World War III was closing in. For years fate had cultivated two antagonists, each with a world mission, each completely righteous, and finally set them on a collision course.

"Were you able to hear the President's statement to the Soviet Union?" Doctor Harper asked.

"Every word," she replied. It had seemed to her the stuff of which coronaries were made.

The President's speech from Camp David had been made on July 12th. Cindy heard it relayed over the BBC the following day. The BBC commentator had first noted an air of crisis in Washington which, he speculated, might have contributed to the speech's intensity. The elections were less than four months away.

Even over the tiny transistor radio with its fading batteries the President's voice had mounted to an emotional peak. "I call upon the Chairman of the Supreme Soviet . . ." Cindy had begun trying to jot it down word for word, to tell the others back in the dorm, ". . . to halt and eliminate the clandestine, reckless, and provocative threat to world security . . ." She quickly fell behind and had to paraphrase as best she could. ". . . accord between our two nations . . . accusing finger point at the Soviet Union rather than Saudi Arabia . . . Saudis the victim of the situation . . . should American citizens be murdered . . . obliged in behalf of American people to take steps . . . protect survivors . . ." Cindy wrote no more. The message was clear. There had been no official response from the Saudis or from the Soviet Union. These immense imponderables touched Cindy far less than her father's reaction.

The Ambassador had listened to the radio with her. Pale, half-smiling at first, he began to look so exhausted that Cindy had touched his arm, saying, "Dad, are you okay?"

"I don't really know, sweetheart," he said, glancing at her so that his face caught the sunlight through the stacks of books.

"Dad, are you crying?"

"Not for years, honey." He sounded hoarse. "When I feel tears coming on, I write a report."

"Yes, you are," she said. It was like being in the presence of a stranger, and she wasn't sure if the stranger was herself or her father, looking so tired and old, with tears in his eyes.

"I've never seen you lose your optimism," she said.

"I wish I had some of your confidence, kiddo," he said. "If I had, I'd have joined a traveling carnival. But then I don't suppose you'd ever have been born."

"Do you think there'll be a war, Dad?"

"I don't know, honey, but as Churchill said, 'the terrible ifs begin to accumulate.' "

"You're talking about the President's speech, right?"

"Only partly. They used to call that sort of talk 'brinksmanship.' That's just a sophisticated diplomatic term for a teenage game called 'chicken.' All you need for that is a straight road with a white line down the middle, a couple of cars, and a couple of fools at the wheels. They dash at each other down that line till the one with better sense swerves away. He's the chicken. The Saudis would say he'd lost face. So would we. So would the Russians. Still, it's a punk's game, 'chicken' is, but when politicians begin to play, risking millions of lives, they're cheered for their statesmanship and steady nerves."

"It can't be that foolish, Dad. I mean, you can't blame the leaders for everything."

"I suppose you're right. As a matter of fact, I don't know whether the leaders lead or are pushed along by the crowd behind them. I've been in the foreign service all my adult life, and I've seen so many wars. They all seemed vitally important at the time, and now I can't remember why they started. You'll forgive me for speechifying, old dear, but I don't get much chance these days. Do we fight for living space or to make the world safe for democracy? Or for two full gas tanks in every garage? I've read that men fight to impress their mothers. You tell me. I'm getting too old to know, kiddo, and the way things are going, pretty soon I won't even care."

JULY 15TH. I haven't seen Kim in a couple of days, not even from a distance. He doesn't use the radio anymore. I should try and help him. I know it's cowardly not to. The U.N. is trying to find a face-saving solution for everybody—that's our big hope. Salim is becoming a problem. Up until now, his shyness has protected me from getting involved, but I don't know how long it will last. He said this morning, after we'd all heard the news about the U.N., that it would be a sadness for him, because it would mean losing me. I said I'd write and all that, but it didn't cheer him up. I even remembered (at last!) to give him the postage stamps and he looked more down in the mouth than ever. "I am not selfish as you think," he said. "I would not hold you against your will." But it wasn't just what he said, but how he said it. You would have thought I was some sort of queen, beloved but baffling.

JULY 16TH. Gift day. Did I do the right thing this time? Salim showed up with a plush little box and said, "For you, Cindy." I opened the box. "They are not large, but very good quality." He was talking about diamond earrings!

Cindy snapped the box closed and handed it to Salim. "I can't accept them," she said. "I'm very flattered, Salim, but no, I can't."

"Please, Cindy, you will do me a great honor," he said quietly.

"Salim, if a girl takes an expensive present like that, it means only one thing." At least, she thought, he isn't like Kim. He didn't lunge at her and he kept his voice down.

"Surely it is not a bad thing."

"In a place like this, with nothing to do but gossip? I can just hear my mom."

A spot of red appeared on both his cheeks. Then he mumbled, "Cindy, I want to live with you and die with you."

Cindy was beginning to feel out of her depth. "Please, Salim, no more talk of dying."

"Everything with you, Cindy."

"Salim, that's very sweet of you, but . . ."

"It is hurting me for you to say that."

"All right, if you want, I'll wear them when you're around. I'll pretend the earrings are mine. But honestly, Salim, for a clever guy you have a lot to learn," she told him.

"You are confusing me, Cindy. What have I done?"

She held up her hands to him as though they were once again tied together. "I'm a prisoner here, remember? And you're a guard, bringing me tempting presents. But I'm still here by force. You can't force a person into falling for you, even with a sugar coating. Maybe you're a terrific person, but to me you're a kidnapper first. Now you'd like to tempt me into a harem or something, but, believe me, I'm not the harem type."

"There are no harems among my people. You and I, we could go to the desert."

Cindy had a vision of the sands of The Empty Quarter,

of slouching back and forth on a lumbering camel. Actually, it didn't sound that bad, she thought. Better than the Embassy, anyway. But she dared not cross such a threshold into the unknown even if it did not mean abandoning her family and her Americanness. Salim seemed to sense this fear, for he said, "We could go to your country, to that New England your mother speaks of."

"You'd hate it there."

"I would hate it more without you. Say you will come with me, Cindy."

"How would it really be, Salim? Would we ride off into the sunset on a camel and live happily ever after? It's so easy to say so."

Salim looked at her with suspicion, as if she were only making excuses. "The Rashid have no more camels. A cousin would meet us outside the Embassy in his truck. A very nice truck, with air conditioning."

That killed the daydream right there.

"Do you think I would desert my parents? Or Kim, in his state?"

"You are not his keeper, surely."

"But I feel responsible. He has no one at all now. Besides, if the U.N. doesn't do something soon, the President will, I suspect before your cousin could get here with his truck."

"If Allah so wills," Salim agreed grudgingly.

"So why not a grand gesture? Why doesn't your General Aziz let us go while he can still make a few points?"

"If it were up to me," Salim said, "I would say yes. But who knows, I may have been corrupted in my thinking by your Western ideas. I have told you about our sense of honor. To give in to pressure would blacken one's face. A true believer would say, 'Do what you will, American President, we have one weapon left: our lives, our willingness to die.' "

So they were back to that again. Cindy walked down the aisle of books in the library and looked out the fly-spattered window toward the outer wall where a guard prowled. Salim came after her. "Cindy, what's wrong? What can I do?"

"Be funny, for a change. You're always so serious. Tell me a joke to make me laugh."

"I don't know any," he pleaded.

"Oh, come on, try. I bet you know all sorts of dirty jokes. Think hard."

"Even if I knew one, I would not repeat it in your presence," Salim said indignantly.

"Be a sport."

"They're between men, Cindy."

"All right, if you don't tell one, I will. You want to hear a really gross story?" She was practically shouting in his face. "About the little old lady who wants to have her dead lovebirds stuffed?"

"Cindy, please. Tell me what you want. I'll buy you anything."

> JULY 17TH. Now I've done it. The worst part is, it was exciting. Some of it was fun, except toward the end, which spoiled everything as usual. But why am I behaving this way? If I could be back at school or in the States reading this, I wouldn't believe it. This isn't the real me anymore, it's some kind of nut who doesn't know what's good for her or when to stop. The world's coming apart, Mom and Dad are depressed, Kim won't even speak to me, and I can't wait for this freaked-out Arab to turn up. Am I just bored and trying to torment him? Or am I really excited by him? The whole situation's so weird I really don't know.

She was in the library, ready to turn on the radio, when Salim came up behind her and, without a word, threw himself at her with an ecstatic groan. Suddenly they were wrestling, wedged up against the book stacks. "Salim, no, don't!" but her confused words seemed to encourage him. He was kissing her very roughly and clumsily, but she didn't resist until he tried to slip a hand down her cotton slacks. She couldn't pull away but she brought her right knee up, hard. Salim let go and curled up in a ball on the floor.

Cindy bent over him. "I'm sorry, Salim. Are you in one piece?"

"Forgive me," he groaned, gritting his teeth, "but somehow I thought . . . I hoped . . ."

"It's nobody's fault," she assured him seriously. "Salim, you're very attractive. I might fall for you, too, but not in this place. I couldn't fall in love with you or anyone here, not ever. But I know you're my friend and you'd never do anything to hurt me. You wouldn't, would you?"

"I only wish to be with you."

"I'm at your mercy, Salim, and I know I'm awfully lucky you're so decent about, well, not taking advantage. Only promise me."

"It won't happen again, Cindy."

"I'm not as strong as you. I'm a prisoner. You could do what you like that way, but if you ever try it, I would never speak one word to you again. I would not respect you, Salim. Never." He might have been tied to a stake the way he stood there, his chin down. "Salim, look, I'd like you to kiss me in a nice gentle way. I would." He looked up finally with a puzzled expression, half-smiling.

"Please," he whispered.

Cindy made herself relax until his grasp grew so strong her fingers spread apart and stiffened. Her eyes did not close but opened wide. Then Salim suddenly released her, saying, "I'm sorry. I didn't mean to do that."

"I didn't say anything."

"I must have hurt you."

"A little," Cindy admitted, "but I'm tough."

"I'm sorry, Cindy."

"Don't keep saying you're sorry." She locked her hands around the back of his neck. "More like this. That's lots better." They stood there for a long moment, embraced, then Cindy drew back. She met no resistance.

"This is good," Salim said.

"See, I told you it was . . ." There was something different about the shadows at the end of the aisle of books. A dark bar had fallen across the floor. Cindy tried to convince herself that it was only the guard eavesdropping as she tiptoed down the aisle. The shadow never moved and as she turned the corner there stood Kim with a frozen and insane look on his face, as if he'd been standing there for hours.

"Cindy," Kim said quietly, but it was as though a blast of heat came from him and struck her. As he turned on Salim, he seemed to swell and grow taller. He stiffened his right hand in a karate gesture. "You bastard!" he hissed.

Salim swung his gun around on its strap and the bolt clicked. "Would you kiss the edge of the sword?" he challenged Kim. The blue barrel of the submachine gun was steady in his grip. "The mechanism is very simple," Salim said, aiming at Kim's chest. "You depress the trigger, and bullet after bullet comes out."

For a moment a stubborn hatred flickered in Kim's eyes. Then he took a step back. His hands fell to his sides. Salim tipped the gun forward so that it aimed toward the floor.

What happened next might have seemed funny if it weren't so deadly serious. All three took great gulps of air like a trio of divers surfacing. Then Kim reached for the radio. "That's mine," he said. For a thoughtful moment he held it in both hands, then suddenly smashed it against the metal frame of the bookcase.

"Thank you," Salim said contemptuously. "Soon I would have been forced to report it. Yes, thank you." Then he looked at Cindy and held out his hand. "I'm leaving. Come." He sounded so sure and possessive she shook her head no, and for a moment he hesitated as if unsure whether to force the issue. Then he turned and left, alone.

For the first time since the day his father had been killed, Cindy had a chance to really look at Kim. He was trembling like someone with a fever. She half-expected him to vomit. "I'm not kidding," he said very slowly and carefully. "That wog wants to decorate his harem with you. He loves you like he loves a good carpet."

Cindy felt like telling Kim that he was talking his usual crock of nonsense but he looked so weird she was a little afraid of him. "Oh, come on, Kim, let's be friends again. Kim?" She took hold of his hands and then noticed his fingernails. They looked as though they'd been gnawed back to the quick by yellow rot.

"Oh, Kim, what have you done to your poor hands? You have such nice fingers."

He began laughing, but there was no mirth in it, rather a violent, nervous insincerity. "Regression to the infantile," he said. "Ha, ha, the infant expressing rage at poor crazy Mom, at his goddamn wet diapers, ha, ha, at his father who got himself chopped in two, ha, ha, ha."

"Stop it, Kim. Stop it!" She'd heard you were supposed to slap people when they got hysterical but she didn't dare, he looked so violent.

"Am I going to pieces?" he said, questioning himself, not Cindy. Her expression must have answered him for he gave her an odd look, and there was something in his face that was so wild it made her afraid, the look of an animal that doesn't think of itself or anything else, only of what it wants.

"If I'm going to pieces, I'm not going alone," Kim threatened, his words pure menace. His fists clenched, he left the library.

For several minutes Cindy stood there, leaning her head against the cool dusty books, breathing deeply. She could speak to her father, but he had enough to worry about now, and she knew he'd been to see Kim a few times since his father's death. No, if anyone should deal with Kim it should be herself, and she didn't have the courage. All she did was pick up the broken radio and put it back in the Bible. She had the feeling she'd just witnessed the signing of a death warrant.

"Take a breather, Cindy," Doctor Harper said, and then into the microphone, "End of CRC 9." He turned off the recorder, ejected the cassette, and inserted a new one. Then he sat on the edge of the bed, confidential, seeking an ally in the unraveling of a mystery. "It comes down to this, Cindy. They don't know what went wrong when the United Nations seemed to have the situation in hand. Why were people killed the day the U.N. delegation arrived?"

"I'm supposed to tell you?" Cindy asked in surprise.

"All they want is information," said Harper, "not a confession."

Putting the clues together, Cindy had concluded that she was on a Russian submarine. On guard, she meant to answer neither no nor yes to his questions. No sooner had she so resolved than Cindy had the distinct and uncomfortable feeling that Doctor Harper knew exactly how she felt.

"I thought we were friends, Cindy," Harper said, wondering at her sudden withdrawal. "Now you suddenly seem hostile. Why is that?"

She evaded with, "Wouldn't you be, by now?"

"I suppose, but with any luck we only have to get through today. It all boils down to this session. Once we know what happened when the U.N. delegation arrived, that's it. Then we can take our time with your rehabilitation. Are you up to it? Please try, for your own sake." He clicked on the recorder. "Cindy?"

"I'm a blank on all that, really."

Doctor Harper smiled uncertainly. "Cindy," he said, "would you like to know what I suspect?" She had been caught, she knew it, like a clumsy thief pointing a water pistol at a bank teller. "Cindy?" Doctor Harper leaned closer, grasped her wrist. "Please don't lie. It makes it so much harder if you do."

Cindy pulled away, hunched up defensively against the metal headboard. He was right, she did not intend to help. On the other hand, she was being honest, in that all she could recall of those last days was a volcano of upsurging images that were terrifying but without coherence. Behind her eyes she could stare into that thunderous inferno, a twilight full of bright stabbings, but only the terror made sense. Better to be tortured here and now as long as she need not probe, as long as she could remain snug in that private place within herself. There, it was still and safe, a place to hide without fear or pain.

"Would it help, Cindy, if I started off with some questions?"

She shook her head. "I doubt it."

"You must try. Either that, or we may have to give your

memory a jog. I'd rather not approach it that way but . . . You don't have to answer right away. Think about it."

Think about it. Cindy stared straight ahead, her heart beating off the seconds.

There was no more discussion. "I'll be back," Doctor Harper said, and left the room. Cindy drew knees up defensively against her chest. She put her fist to her mouth and cried silently. She had to call on a Cindy Cooper who might not exist. "Oh, Dad," she whispered to herself, "please give me a piece of your courage. I'm so scared."

Presently Doctor Harper returned, with what looked like a newspaper under his arm. "I hate to see that look, Cindy," he said.

"I'm afraid," she said.

"Of what?"

"Of what's going to happen."

"Cindy, I'm not the Grand Inquisitor; I'm your doctor. I'm sorry you're reluctant to cooperate. Under the circumstances, it may only be natural. In any case, you've made it necessary for me to show you something." It was a relief to be talked to, and not about. "I want you to read this. It won't be very pleasant but . . ." She sat before him, chin up, eyes closed with an air of sacrificial bravery as if presenting her slender throat to her executioner. "Open your eyes, Cindy."

He held out the Paris edition of the *Herald Tribune*. At first Cindy stared blankly at the black staccato slashes of ink, not putting the letters together. Finally they formed words, then sentences screamed at her: RESCUE ATTEMPT FAILS: MASSACRE AT U.S. EMBASSY. Her eyes darted down the page, picking up bits and pieces. OPERATION LIGHTNING BOLT . . . 10 C-150 ATLAS TRANSPORTS ABORT . . . THREE

SEA LION HELICOPTERS LOST . . . "Congressional Medal of Honor winner Colonel James Hagedorn among missing . . . only known survivor . . ." and here Cindy's frantic glance riveted ". . . Cynthia Cooper, the daughter and only child of Ambassador Howard Cooper . . . in protective custody for intensive medical care and debriefing . . . a true American heroine . . ." Why! Why! What had she done except survive? Cindy looked toward Doctor Harper for help, her eyes silently pleading.

"I'm terribly sorry, Cindy. If there'd been another way . . . Do you want anything? Want to walk around?"

Just then she couldn't have stood on two feet. Inside her mind it was all so vivid, so horribly clear, and yet totally confusing. She could see the smoke sagging in murky strands. There'd been a peppery smell burning her nostrils and she could feel the heat of the flames, thunderous plumes of fire, and over its sucking roar she could hear the whomp-whomp of great rotors. Looking up, she'd seen three helicopters dipping and gliding toward the Embassy like khaki-colored frisbees. She had caught a glimpse then of her mother running, her nightgown transparent in the beam of the spotlights, the curlers in her hair forming an iridescent crown. Then the rotors had come again and the flames threw red flakes that swirled upward so that the moon seemed to withdraw from the heat. Cindy looked for her mother, but she had disappeared. Cindy felt herself plunging into deep black space that seemed deeper than regret or pain or sorrow.

"I see it's coming back to you," Doctor Harper observed.

"No. Nothing. Nothing's coming back," Cindy insisted. "I know this sort of thing. You can have newspapers like this made to order on Times Square. What a disgusting joke." She tried to force a scornful laugh. It was closer to tears. "I know you're Russian. You are, aren't you? That accounts for the accent, doesn't it? And keeping me locked in here without any visitors. Not my parents or anyone."

"Cindy, you poor kid. You've had a hell of a shock, but we'll see this through, you and I."

"You! What do you mean, you!" He was Judas Iscariot just then, and the rage that burst in her welled up fierce and triumphant. Cindy screamed at him, hammered at him. Then, as Doctor Harper backed off, she began tearing at the bandage on her left wrist.

"Oh, no, we can't have you hurting yourself." Harper dove to confine her hands and again she flailed at him until he bore her arms down. Finally her resistance collapsed. There were canvas straps attached to the sides of the bed and Harper began to fasten them over her. She laughed out loud, a shrill gust of fragile laughter, until with a groan she gave up and her eyes overflowed with tears.

11

Remembering was not only agonizing, but wrong, for it meant that if the details returned to her there was only the enemy to take note of them. Cindy made her position clear to Doctor Harper. He had given her an injection, and she was no longer hysterical but still feared him.

"I'm sorry you think that, Cindy," he replied. "I'm not a Russian, but let's suppose it were true. Say I'm an agent for the Soviet KGB. Does it matter?" She offered no response, no longer wanted to look at the man who called himself Doctor Harper. "Tell me, Cindy, why should it matter? If I were a Russian, wouldn't I also seek a way out?"

"A way out of what?"

"Out of a world crisis of confrontation. Listen, Cindy, it may already be too late. There are reports—unconfirmed—that Soviet forces have entered Yugoslavia. You see, I have my own theory about the Embassy affair, that it may have been one of those peculiar cases totally unrelated to international politics. What do you think?"

Cindy did not think so much as feel, with the creeping fear of being in an alien world while her own was drifting away beyond recall. In this strange white room, things were going out of joint.

"Let me give you a hypothetical case, Cindy," Harper

rambled on. "There are two superpowers, opposed to each other and equal in strength. All their arguments toward a peaceful solution of a situation have been placed on a scale, and it remains in balance. Then suppose one last fact is disclosed, a fact that may of itself have no more weight than a feather, or for analogy's sake, say a straw. Suppose, for instance, it were discovered that General Aziz wasn't behind the assault on the United Nations' delegation. That might have no more weight than a straw in the wind, but remember, it was a straw that broke the camel's back. Why are you smiling, Cindy?"

"Nothing. I just thought that might account for there not being any camels in Arabia."

Harper looked puzzled, wondering if he had missed something. "In any event," he continued, "it might be enough to initiate one last diplomatic gesture, provide an excuse for everyone, both sides, to save face. I can only hypothesize, but you might just possibly supply that straw I've been talking about. So you see, whether I'm CIA or KGB really makes very little difference."

He was very clever, Cindy had to admit, but the more persuasive his argument, the more determined she was to resist.

Harper waited to see the impact of his argument. When she made no response he seemed to shrink. "Very well," he said, "this will help with the amnesia."

"No, please," Cindy whispered as the doctor approached with the syringe, "not another one." She struggled against the confining straps.

"That was just a tranquilizer, Cindy. This is a derivative of sodium amytal—it makes most people feel marvelous."

Cindy flung her head sideways on the pillow and stared at the white wall. She tried to imagine a range of high, snow-covered mountains. Switzerland: she willed her thoughts to be far away while there was still time. The needle pierced her arm. She began to sweat. A drowsy indolence began to gnaw at her will to resist. Every part of her wanted to sleep but she knew she must stay awake, alert to what the doctor was trying to make her do. "I'm back at school," she told herself. "I'm at Le Rosey and it's snowing. Everything's white." Slowly she withdrew into a tiny secret hiding place that was secure and warm and far from the reach of reality and its threats.

The only trouble was, Doctor Harper went with her, staring at her so intently that he gave the illusion of stealthily drawing closer. Is that me laughing? How strange. Why am I doing that?

"Feeling better?" Harper asked, and his words came as though through an echo chamber. "Good, now let's see what we can do."

She'd done her best, she'd been brave. Her father would have approved. She'd held out against them pretty well, hadn't she? If only someone would tell her so. "Dad, did I do all right?" and her father answered soothingly with Doctor Harper's voice, "Just fine, sweetheart. Only tell the truth now. You can rely on others to tell lies," and her own voice answering, "I'll try, Dad, if that's what you say." The odd thing was, she wasn't sure whether she was just thinking or speaking aloud, or actually living through those last hours at the Embassy with the dispassionate interest of one seeing history revealed on a movie screen.

There were the helicopters again, swinging low over the rooftops. Now one of them was disabled and billowing smoke. It fluttered off by itself. "Cindy, hurry!" Salim tugged at her elbow, steering her across the palm court that heaved underfoot like a pot of boiling oatmeal. "This way, hurry!" A string of heavy dull bumps followed as they ran into an acrid yellow fog where vague figures groped aimlessly. There followed a closer burst that threw out sharp orange flashes and a churning wave of pink and gray force that knocked her down. Walls crumbled around them as Salim pulled her toward a building where the windows blazed. Smoke streamed from the upper sills like escaping rats. "We can't go in there!" she screamed at Salim. "It's on fire!" And he'd kept pulling her, yelling back, "It's the only place to go!"

12

"Cindy, you're doing beautifully," Doctor Harper said, "but it's not the rescue business we need to fill in on, it's the United Nations visit. Just let it come."

"You want to hear about the U.N.," she repeated. Here lay the terrible core of it all, and yet with the injection—Doctor Harper had given her another one—Cindy felt detached, like a medical student witnessing abdominal surgery.

"Please, Cindy, from the beginning, when you first heard the news."

> JULY 23RD. A miracle! The U.N. has broken the deadlock and the Secretary General is coming to Saudi Arabia to mediate. General Aziz and the King have pledged good faith.

After all the days of suspense and rumor in which war and continued captivity had seemed inevitable, it was almost too good to be true, and she wanted to confirm the news with her parents. But her mother was beyond caring. She was sick of the heat, she said, and the dreary food and the filthy wogs. She wasn't speaking to her husband. Cindy's father, on the other hand, was guardedly optimistic. "Some people will feel cheated," he mused. "All those lovely expensive rockets and tanks ready to shoot, and now they have to go back on the shelf. Let's hope so, anyway."

Things were looking so good, with the ceasefire and the United Nations coming the following day, that General Aziz had ordered a feast for the Americans. Cindy presumed it was to make them feel more like honored guests than prisoners. Whatever, it was quite grand. Persian carpets and low tables were set up Bedouin-style around the palm court. With the electricity shut down, the court wasn't lit in the usual way, from above, but by bright stabbing carbide lamps that stood on the ground. They cast up violet shadows into the palms, not exactly flattering but exotic. At first the Americans had a hard time trying to act like old friends with their guards. They were like actors mumbling their lines. They tried to use Arabic, "Salam alaikum," and the guards came back with pidgin English, "And how do you do this evening?" Fortunately, the food arrived quickly, so they could stop play-acting. Servants staggered out with all sorts of platters. There were awesome brass trays heaped with rice and lamb, head and all—which, Cindy thought, was really gross. There was other meat stuffed with macaroni and hard-boiled eggs, more her style. No one could say General Aziz was a stingy host, which was about the worst thing you could say about an Arab. The food was so rich, compared with what they'd been eating for months, it made Cindy feel queasy, and when one of the secretaries told her that what she'd been stuffing herself with was baby camel, she nearly threw up.

Cindy would remember it, though, as a pleasant if intense evening, except for Kim being there. He'd been staying in his dorm, not even coming to the cafeteria for meals. His roommates had permission to take him food or he might have starved to death. This night he put in a public appearance, sitting down at a table across the court. Did he mean to avoid her because he looked so awful, all hunched up and scruffy? Of course none of the prisoners were exactly *Vogue* material at this point, but Cindy remembered Kim as always having been particularly clean and well groomed. Perhaps it was the carbide lamps that made his eyes look so glittery and wild. Cindy wasn't sure. She steeled herself to speak to him, but a good chance didn't come. Only a few people were still eating when someone clapped his hands and a tall Arab, who reminded her too much for comfort of Colonel Anderson's executioner, strode around with a large bottle of Chanel perfume and splashed it on all their greasy hands. Cindy looked over to where Kim had been but he seemed to have vanished, which put an end to her intention of catching him afterward. The perfume signaled the official end of the party, except for the speeches.

General Aziz, reminding her a bit of the jolly bird man of Christmas Eve, began by saying, "Allah, may his wisdom be praised, has brought us through a time of trial and travail. Now all is well. Old wounds have a chance to heal." At the end he raised a cup of coffee and said, "To my American friends and to the United States of America, long may she wave," which caused a double take or two, but no one dared to laugh.

Then Ambassador Cooper stood up. He'd spent years putting nervous people at their ease, and he had an air of really professional sincerity. "Tonight," he said, "I am not an American. I am not a New Englander. I feel I am a citizen of the world. We are one family here tonight. I only hope that the leaders who will presently be coming together will do so in this spirit. Then perhaps if they are strong enough to make circumstances serve, they will have the strength to trust one another and be able to break the sword that hangs above us all. If not, may God have mercy on the human race."

> It was a terrifically upbeat and optimistic evening, only something spoiled it at the end. When I got back to my room I saw right away that somebody had been through my suitcases. At first I suspected my roommates—there's been lots of "borrowing"—but nothing was missing. Only the little glass camel Kim gave me was broken, not in two or three pieces, but really pulverised. Why? I hate the idea of anyone going through my things, particularly the thought of Kim sneaking in here to do such a nasty, weird thing. I'm sorry for him, too, but what can I do to help?

On this note Cindy concluded her observations for July 23rd, 1988. It was the last entry that she would make in the diary.

Since the news of the United Nations, Cindy had not seen Salim. She had begun to wonder if he had left the Embassy compound. It would have been easier, under the circumstances, but unexpectedly he turned up at the dorm the following morning. She greeted him rather coolly, having no intention of taking up where they'd left off.

"You should be happy, Cindy. Soon you will go home."

"Do you believe that, Salim? I want to believe it."

"There is a saying that the words of the night are coated with butter, and when the sun shines they melt away. Still, General Aziz says you will go home. Yes, I believe it. Would you like to see the U.N. delegation? The General will receive them, and I can arrange it."

"Here?"

"Right here. And your father. It is all arranged." Salim smiled. "That is good news, yes? I told you, Cindy, you would not be hurt."

"We're not home yet," she replied.

"Oh, Cindy, if the General had sentenced everyone to death I would have saved you. My life for yours. We Arabs have our foolish pride. Come, they will be here soon. It is a great thing."

"Suppose everyone had been sentenced to death," Cindy asked. "Would you have killed the others?"

"It would not have been my job."

"Just suppose. You always carry a gun."

"But Cindy," Salim protested, "I have never used it. It is for me only an embarrassment."

"What if Kim hadn't stopped that time?"

"Thanks be to Allah, he did stop. So we don't know. Come, or we will be late and see nothing."

Cindy had not visited the Embassy's entrance hall since the day of her arrival months before. All around the balcony where she and Salim waited were hung the flags of many nations. General Aziz and Ambassador Cooper stood together in the hall below, surrounded by other dignitaries and reporters with TV cameras and microphones. What surprised Cindy most was that the Marine guards were back on duty, interspersed with neatly uniformed Saudis. Outside, a crowd in the street had begun to cheer, and the only black lining to this otherwise silvery cloud was Kim Anderson. Cindy had noticed him from the corner of her eye. He stood toward the back of the crowd that now packed the balcony.

Just then the first of several limousines turned in at the main gate. Cindy pressed forward to see. She forgot Kim in the upsurge of excitement until he had elbowed his way beside her. His eyes, blazing red and homicidal, seemed actually to give out light. "Kim!" she said, as if sharp words might hold him back. "What do you want?" With his hands raised, the fingernails gnawed back to bloody stumps, he seemed about to seize her by the throat. Then Salim turned half around. A ray of sun lit the barrel of his gun. It glowed pearly gray and Kim went for it instead. Salim was caught by surprise but got one hand on the gun as Kim gave it a spiraling twist. The leather strap held firm, pinning Salim's other arm to his side. Kim's weight forced him back against the marble railing.

In the excitement generated by the confrontation below, this scuffle had thus far been taken as simply part of the wider enthusiasm. Only Cindy recognized it for what it was, a death struggle, and not being of a temperament to stand by with hands pressed to a stricken face, she leaped, trying to separate them. She felt Kim's fingers closing painfully on her shoulder. If nothing else she had divided his assault. The three of them were locked together, their feet scuffling on the slippery floor as if performing an absurd dance. From the railing they lurched back against the wall. Kim's face strained, the tendons of his neck protruding as he made a final effort to tear the gun away. Three pairs of hands had closed on it now, straining back and forth, until Kim wrenched backward with all his weight. Then the oiled metal slid through Cindy's fingers until they caught on a protrusion, held briefly, and then gave way, caught on something else that bent back. Only when the submachine gun bucked and boomed and she saw Kim reeling backward did she realize it had been the trigger. At least one bullet had caught him in the chest, expelling a loud "Hah!" from his lungs. For an instant the wall held him erect, and then he slid to the floor, face canted forward, open mouthed, eyes narrowly regarding a crimson blot that spread down his shirt front.

How many bullets had issued from that submachine gun no one ever knew. At first it was not even certain which side had opened fire, the Marines or the Arab guards, let alone who had given the command. For a moment the great echoing room had fallen silent in perplexed horror, like so many visitors at a zoo who had inadvertantly wandered into the lion's cage. Then firing became general. Bodies leaped or were flung down.

With a sinking agony Cindy realized what had happened. The air was a red-and-black blur and when Salim hauled at her arm, her feet seemed stuck to the floor, stuck in it. He yanked her into motion. Without ever sensing a transition she was running blindly. In a doorway her shoulder hit the jamb. She spun half round, found her feet as Salim never let go until they arrived at the abandoned library. There they clung to each other like two drowning swimmers who had somehow helped each other ashore. They leaned together, trembling with fatigue and bewilderment. I killed him, Cindy told herself. He needed help and I killed him. She wanted to scream until her lungs were bloody. She glanced up at Salim and though neither spoke aloud each told the other countless things, and if her own gaze held terrible questions, she read dark and fearful answers in his eyes.

"I killed him," Cindy finally said aloud.

"Cindy, he killed himself. It was the will of Allah. Do not blame yourself."

Perhaps, and yet she would never forgive herself, "not if I live to be a hundred."

"I'm not sure we have to worry about old age," Salim replied. "Surely now your planes must come, if America is to save face."

In a few minutes everything had changed, yet nature paid no heed. Outside the sky remained blue. The sun scorched down.

Doctor Harper's lips had moved silently with Cindy's as though to help draw out the events at the Embassy that she so laboriously described. When she fell silent he put his hands to his face and drew them slowly down. He was terribly tired.

"Is that it, Cindy?" he asked, and receiving no reply he directed a last remark to the recorder and closed down tape CRC 10. They had come to the end of it.

"Thank you, Cindy," he said. "You don't know how sorry I am, old girl." He was addressing someone who no longer listened, and if he'd been asked whether she ever would find her way out of the nightmare they had just explored together, he could not have given a sure answer.

More important, his suspicion that the crisis at the Embassy was not international in nature had been confirmed. Nudged by a romantic triangle, not even that, the world once more was poised for war. It was only one minor incident among many, no more than a straw that the world might grasp before taking the plunge, but it was all he had.

13

Three hundred feet below the surface of the Indian Ocean, Cynthia Cooper lay alone in the sick bay of the Trident submarine *Nathan Hale*, immobilized by the canvas straps that tightly crossed her arms, chest, and legs. Vaguely, she felt that she had told everything to a Soviet agent. She had tried to be brave, but she had given away secrets. She wanted forgiveness. She wanted her father to say it was all right, but she would never see him again. They were all part of a fragmented and bleeding world, and she had helped to make it so. Better she should be dead and they should live, but there was no going back, she knew that. Was this, then, the destiny she had so smugly awaited, to be the witness, the one who must always relive those last fiery hours that now burned so bright inside her head?

Once again she and Salim were fleeing to the Embassy library, to slump there among the stacks, shocked beyond the capacity for further action. The sound of gunfire gradually subsided as the sunlight crawled across the floor toward evening. Then somewhere on the outskirts of Riyadh a distant siren began to wail. Lost in the stupor of their own thoughts, they paid no attention until, with dusk, came the heavy pulse of helicopters approaching. Abruptly, Salim was on his feet. He ran to a window, ran back. Grabbing Cindy's arm, he pulled her up. "We must leave this place. Hurry!" Cindy shook her head, resisting as he thrust her forward. "The Embassy is mined. It will never be given up to force. Trust me now."

Already they were too late. Explosions shook the air, and a yellow fog wallowed over the tennis courts. The recent grave had erupted into a crater, and bodies lay about in twisted postures. Figures reeled like drunkards out of the wall of smoke. With his hand locked onto her upper arm, Salim propelled her through the palm court and toward the Chancellery. "I have keys," he said as they dashed inside. A number of carbide lamps left over from General Aziz's feast were stored there, and with shaking hands Salim lit two, which cast blade-edged shadows as they ran down the echoing stairs to the basement. The thunderous noises were muffled below ground, and when they reached the glass room, Cindy was not entirely surprised. "General Aziz meant this to be his personal conference chamber," Salim explained. "Come, we'll be safe here."

With the door closed behind them, the sounds of explosions diminished to a whisper, but Cindy still felt the building shudder. Salim drew the padded conference chairs together around the heavy table, and like children playing games they huddled underneath it.

I'll wake up soon, Cindy kept telling herself. Though she knew it was no nightmare, her emotions were in complete suspension. Terrible things had happened. People had died. She was in part responsible and she should be feeling grief and fear and pain, yet she felt none of these. She yawned, one great jaw-straining yawn after another. Salim yawned back at her, a grotesque duet, until Cindy wondered aloud, "With no electricity, is any air getting in here?" Had they sealed themselves in a killing box?

"Wait, Cindy. I will open the door," Salim said, and crawled out from under the table. She watched his dark silhouette groping with the latch when suddenly the glass room was lit by a fierce light. As though struck by a cyclonic gale the glass walls billowed inward, then separated into a shower of jagged ice. Salim was flung back like a rag doll and for a ghastly instant Cindy saw his face, cheeks, chin, lips all laid open to the bone by the splintering shower. Then the concussion from the blast took her as well. She felt herself somersaulting, caught in a cartwheeling universe where everything was black.

At first Cindy thought she was unconscious. She lay in the darkness trying to catch her breath while a plaintive voice whispered, "I'm hurt, Salim. I've hurt myself. Where are you?" and was surprised to realize the voice was her own. The carbide lamps had been snuffed out. The blast had left no lingering flicker of flame to help her assess the situation. She felt bruised all over, and her left arm had been slashed by the glass. "Salim, where are you?" she called again. Only then did she hear his answering voice. "Miss Cindy . . . I'm coming. I'll protect you." Something was dragging and groping toward her. A damp hand touched her ankle. "Miss Cindy, don't die," Salim said. His breathing was as harsh as a knife drawn out of a sandy sheath. Then he began to cough. "It's so cold," he said, and she held him close in the blackness while he shivered. Very quickly the blood pumped out of him, while he grew heavier in her arms. She kept wondering in the dumb numb darkness; how can that be? How can he be getting heavier and be losing so much blood? She rocked him close until gradually a roaring and a flaming grew inside her and she dreamed she was back at Le Rosey, in the snow. It was lovely and cold. She shivered with delight, and the delirium was so real that she mistook the blue-shaded lights of the rescue party for night skiiers.

"Hey, it's a live one," a voice said in English. "She looks American . . . give us a hand. She needs blood. . . . What about the other one? . . . Too late for him. Medic!" The voice echoed down the basement corridor to where other blue lights were bobbing. There followed for Cindy a hazy memory of being carried through smouldering ruins, interspersed with the notion that she'd fallen while skiing and somehow damaged herself. She'd been borne steadily aloft by great wings until the inner night had returned and she had finally wakened in the small white room with Doctor Harper smiling down at her.

Now once again, under the impact of shock, exhaustion, and drugs, Cindy relinquished that white refuge for the wintery dream of Le Rosey. She was telling her classmates how she and Kim had played tennis. Then someone asked her, "Were there camels?" and she answered, "Of course." But it wasn't Switzerland anymore. It was the snowlike sands of The Empty Quarter, and one of the camels obligingly knelt for her and said, "Miss Cindy, will you please to mount," and this she did gracefully, with long white robes flowing around her. She had found her destiny, her triumphant army with banners. The camel went slowly at first, then faster into a jolting, jarring trot, and began to buck.

The submarine convulsed underneath the narrow bed to which she was strapped.

The bucking subsided. The camel galloped smoothly, seeming to fly. Cindy saw herself riding a snow-white camel into the golden glitter of the desert, where only hardy things survive.

Lance Harper, M.D., U.S.N., stood in the *Nathan Hale*'s communications center. Batteries of lights blinked off and on and computer screens flickered their enigmatic messages, but his attention and that of the others was riveted to a radar screen upon which a blue green blip moved steadily upward. The radar operator switched the scan to greater and greater range until the blip was lost.

He was too late; probably he had always been too late. The Soviet probe into Yugoslavia had been met and halted by a combined force of Yugoslav troops and U.S. Marines. In Saudi Arabia the King's forces, with massive aid from the United States, had overrun Riyadh. The rebel insurgents were in scattered flight, and the bulk of the Saudi National Guard had swung toward the northern borders, where a Soviet-backed assault from Iraq was expected, but the real thrust had been elsewhere. Pledging to cut out the fascist canker, a massive Soviet armored assault had passed over the border from the German Democratic Republic into West Germany. NATO's Central Army Group, comprised of the West German 2nd and 3rd Corps, as well as the 5th and 7th U.S. Corps, was falling back from Kassel in the north to the Austrian frontier south of Munich. Austria and Switzerland had already declared their neutrality. The Italian government was paralyzed by a communist-led general strike, but Great Britain and France were mobilizing. A statement had been issued from Moscow that the Soviet Union would refrain from the use of nuclear weapons only so long as NATO did likewise. This was a self-serving proposition, based on the fact that Soviet and Warsaw Pact forces were greater and on the less certain premise that

Soviet jet fighters, operating defensively, could counter the NATO forces' greater technological proficiency. By satellite came the President's less specific statement: he pledged to wage war at all costs against a monstrous tyranny, until victory was achieved.

Doctor Harper found himself staring at an empty radar screen. Now he was the only one aboard the submarine with nothing to do. It had been no more than a straw in the wind, really. Knowing wouldn't have changed things in the long run, surely not. Nor would history remember, for history did not like to predicate its great events on such foolishness. And yet, if it had not been the last straw, what else had it been?

A bell rang, and again the deck shuddered so that Lance Harper had to grab for support. Another impersonal blip appeared on the radar screen, an absurdly diminished ghost of the reality it represented—a thirty-four-foot-long thermonuclear rocket with eight independently targeted reentry warheads, each with evasive capacities and with a one hundred-kiloton yield. Driven to the warm blue surface of the Indian Ocean by an explosion of compressed air that caused the huge attack submarine to tremble, the rocket hung for an instant in suspended animation like a huge silvery dolphin that had flung itself into the air for the sheer joy of life. But instead of falling back, the solid propellant took hold and the rocket hurled itself upward, blinding and majestic, with increasing speed. It began to curve north over the Indian Ocean toward the Soviet Union until visual contact was lost and satellite tracking took over.

Harper turned from the blank radar screen. There was nothing more he could do about that. He moved back toward the sick bay. Now there was only one soul he might try to save in a world that seemed bent on self-destruction.